AND THE
FLESH-EATING
MAGGOTS

DISGUSTING DAVE

AND THE FLESH-EATING MAGGOTS

Jim Eldridge

Illustrated by Jonny Ford

A division of Hachette Children's Books

To my wife, Lynne: my muse for ever

Also by Jim Eldridge:

Disgusting Dave and the Farting Dog

Text copyright © 2010 Jim Eldridge
Illustrations copyright ©2010 Jonny Ford

First published in Great Britain in 2010
by Hodder Children's Books

1

A Catalogue record for this book is available from the British Library

ISBN 978 1 444 90011 8

Typeset by Avon DataSet Ltd, Bidford on Avon, Warwickshire
Printed and bound in Great Britain by CPI Bookmarque, Croydon

Hodder Children's Books
A division of Hachette Children's Books
338 Euston Road, London NW1 3BH

An Hachette UK company
www.hachette.co.uk

CHAPTER 1

When I look back on it, I'm not sure which was worse: the maggots, or having mad Aunt Dora staying at our house. I suppose it should be the maggots. After all, maggots that burrow under your skin and eat your flesh are pretty scary. But then, my family is pretty scary as well.

Aunt Dora isn't scary in a bully-like way – not like my gran, or my older sister Krystal, who could both eat people raw for breakfast and would terrify the SAS. My aunt's scary in a nervous way.

To explain, I'd better go back to the beginning and tell you how it all started.

Every class in our school, Olaf Smith Junior School, had to do a display for the Reception Area. This display was made up of parts of different projects. Our class, 6M, was doing a Science Display and my section was The Human Brain. Originally, I'd wanted to do The Human Digestive System, showing how food went in at one end and came out as poo and pee at the other end, but our teacher, Miss Moore, said that having a lump of poo on display in the Reception Area would not show the school in a good light. I pointed out that it was a plastic poo, which I'd got from a joke shop, and not a real one, but Miss Moore said Absolutely Not. So I was forced to choose another topic from my human body project: hence The Human Brain.

FACTOID:
The Human Brain
A human brain is 80% water. 25% of your blood supply goes to your brain.

I thought it would be great to have a real brain on display, even though it wouldn't be a human one, so I'd asked the butcher if he had a sheep's brain he could let me have for my school project, but he said he wasn't allowed to because of Health and Safety Regulations. Miss Moore also said that because of Health and Safety Regulations I wasn't allowed to use a real brain, or anything containing meat. Personally, I thought that was very unfair, especially because my friend Sukijeet was doing her project on insects, and she was allowed to have real insects on display.

When I pointed this out to Miss Moore, she said that Suki's insects were in glass jars. I said that I'd put my brain in a glass jar for the display, but Miss Moore still said no. So instead, I'd been forced to make a brain out of something else. The main thing was, I wanted a brain that wobbled when you touched it, to show how fragile it was. So I'd bought a model brain from a toyshop and then pressed it into clay at school to make a mould. After the clay had hardened, I'd poured this pink jelly-like stuff into the mould, and when it set I had a really good pink model of a brain, which wobbled just like a real one.

I made it even better by painting on blue and red lines to look like veins, just like the model from the

4

toyshop. By the time I'd finished, my brain looked pretty realistic. I know I could have used the model I got from the toyshop, but that would have been cheating. And, anyway, that model didn't wobble like a real brain does.

The only problem with my Wobbly Brain was that it started to melt, so I had to put it in the school fridge in the kitchens with a big note on it, saying, 'Dave Dickens' Brain. Do Not Touch.'

Although it was an excellent model, it still wasn't as good as having a real brain.

'It's so not fair!' I complained to my friend, Paul, as we left school. 'First I'm not allowed to have a poo on display, not even a plastic one! And now I'm not allowed to have a real brain! What sort of Science Display is it supposed to be? How is this country going to train up the next generation of scientists if we're not allowed to get our fingers on a lump of poo or a brain?'

'Miss Moore said I could put my piece of moon rock on display,' said Paul happily.

'You haven't got a piece of moon rock,' I pointed out.

'Well it *looks* like moon rock,' said Paul.

'It's a lump of coal!'

'It *looks* like a lump of coal, but it also looks like a piece of moon rock,' said Paul.

FACTOID:
Moon Rock
The six NASA Apollo missions to the moon's surface brought a total of 326kg of moon rock back to Earth for examination.

When I got home I was still feeling a bit fed up, but I cheered up when Fred bounced out from his kennel to greet me. Fred is my dog. Well, I suppose he's not really *my* dog, he actually belongs to the granny of the bully at our school, the dreadful Banger Bates, who bullied me into looking after Fred while his gran was away on holiday for a week. He did that because Fred had this terrible problem with wind. Fred used to fart, these really massive silent farts which could knock an elephant unconscious, and Banger didn't want to look after Fred and have his house stinking up.

As it turned out, Banger forcing me to look after Fred was one of the best things that ever happened to me, because Fred became my pet and my friend. When I took him back home after that week, his owner, Banger's gran, said I could take Fred for walks whenever I wanted, and a few months ago, she asked if I'd like to look after him all the time because she found caring for a dog hard work at her age. And that's how Fred moved into our house. And that's why I think of him as *my* dog.

At first, Dad and Mum (and my mad, terrifying sister Krystal) weren't keen because Fred still let off the occasional fruity fart that made their eyes water, but not as often as he used to. And I persuaded Dad to get a kennel for him, so Fred spent a lot of his time outside in our garden. Really, Fred only came into the house when I was at home, to sit with me in my room when I was doing my homework, or looking at interesting things under my microscope. He'd already worked out that Krystal didn't like him, so he made sure to stay out of her way as much as he could. For me, this showed how intelligent dogs can be.

FACTOID:
Animal Intelligence
Monkeys and elephants are reckoned to be the most intelligent animals. Elephants can add up and subtract, and young chimpanzees have done better than college students in some number tests.

Anyway, I got home and went through to the garden. Fred came out of his kennel to greet me, wagging his tail, a big smile on his face, which always makes me feel good. I was just giving him a hug when my dreaded sister Krystal came stomping out of the back door.

'That dog farted at me!' she stormed, and pointed

an accusing finger at Fred, just in case I was going to confuse him with any other dog.

'No, he didn't!' I defended him.

'How do you know? You weren't here!' snapped back Krystal.

Fred, meanwhile, had done the intelligent thing and sneaked back into his kennel to be out of sight of the Wrath of Krystal.

'What's going on?' Mum appeared, looking annoyed. 'Whenever you two get together you start arguing!'

'That dog farted at me as I went indoors!' said Krystal angrily, and again she pointed, this time at the kennel.

'I'm sure he didn't do it deliberately,' said Mum, trying to calm things down.

'Exactly,' I said. 'And Fred hardly farts at all these days.'

'He did it on purpose,' insisted Krystal. 'He knows I don't like him. As I came up the path, he turned round and pointed his bum at me and let one go.'

'Now, now,' said Mum, more severely this time. 'I want you two to stop all this arguing.'

I looked at Mum, shocked. Once again, I reflected how unfair life was. Krystal was the one doing all the moaning and starting an argument by picking on me and Fred, and I got accused of being the baddie!

'I wasn't arguing!' I protested.

'Well you are now,' said Mum. 'So stop it!'

I decided there was only one way out of this situation. 'I was just going to take Fred for a walk,' I said.

'Good,' snapped Krystal. 'And while you're out you can get a cork and push it up his—'

'Krystal!' said Mum sternly.

Krystal shut up, but glowered at me.

'Walkies, Fred!' I said, and I went indoors to get his lead.

Little did I know, I'd soon have a lot more to worry about than Fred farting.

CHAPTER 2

That night, Mum went off to one of her evening classes and Krystal went round to her friend Shelly's house. Dad still wasn't home from work, which meant Fred and I had the house to ourselves, which was great. We settled down in the living room in front of the TV and I flicked through the channels looking for something interesting to watch. I found a fantastic documentary about flesh-eating maggots in Africa. It was brilliant!

This fly lays its eggs in wounds on people's skin. After about twelve hours, the eggs hatch into maggots which start feeding on the flesh of the person, burrowing and eating their way further into their body. Sometimes they burrow right through and pop out through the person's skin somewhere else on their body.

I was just watching a maggot munching its way
out of the back of someone's neck when I heard
my dad say: 'Dave?' from the doorway. Because
this documentary was so fascinating, I hadn't heard
him come in. But when I heard him speak my heart
sank. From the way he said my name I knew there
was trouble.

Not 'trouble' as in I was going to get the blame
for something I'd done wrong, like the time I
accidentally left my collection of different sorts

of snot on Gran's kitchen table, or when I was examining vomit from our next-door neighbour's fence under my microscope to find out what had made the person throw up and left my vomity slides in our bathroom. No, this was the voice Dad put on when there was Bad News.

I did my best to pretend I hadn't heard and carried on watching the TV, but he just said, 'Dave?' again, only a bit louder. He didn't actually shout, just sounded Serious But A Bit Louder, which was how I knew it was Really Bad News. I was pretty certain it involved me, and I didn't really want to find out more.

'This is a good programme,' I said, trying to divert his attention away from whatever he was about to say. 'It's about flesh-eating maggots. It's really educational.'

It didn't work. Maybe I should have chosen another subject – something he cared about, like Arsenal FC. Then he might have started talking about them and the goals they'd scored lately instead, and I could have just switched off from listening to him and carried on watching the TV, giving the occasional nod of agreement.

'Dave, we've got a problem,' he said, very seriously.

Oh no! I thought. We've lost all our money and Dad and Mum are going to have to sell the house.

'It's a big problem,' he added, even more seriously, and now I thought: Mum and Dad are getting a divorce, and I wondered which of them I would go and live with. I was just thinking I might prefer to go with Dad, because Krystal would go with Mum and living with her is a nightmare, when Dad said: 'It's your Aunt Dora.'

Aunt Dora? Dad's sister? What could be her problem? Well, lots, to be honest, because Aunt Dora is really nervous and scared of everything on the planet Earth, and possibly things on every other planet in the galaxy as well, including most asteroids. Then it hit me: maybe Aunt Dora was dead! The voice Dad was using was the one he used when telling a person that someone he liked a lot had died. Like my hamster. But I didn't like Aunt Dora.

'She's left your Uncle Pete.'

I looked at Dad, puzzled. So Aunt Dora had left Uncle Pete. So what? I had missed two minutes of a brilliant and exciting programme about flesh-eating maggots just to hear that?

'Oh,' I said. Then I thought I'd better say something else to show I was taking this news as hard as he was, so I added: 'That's sad.'

I went back to watching the maggots, which by now were burrowing their way back into this man's head. Suddenly the screen went blank.

FACTOID:
Parasitic Worms
Tapeworms get inside the human stomach and grow, living off the human being. Some can grow up to forty feet long.

Dad had picked up the remote and turned the TV off. 'I need to talk to you, Dave,' he said. 'This is important and concerns us as a family.'

Desperately I pointed at the screen. 'Those are flesh-eating maggots!'

'You can watch it on iPlayer,' said Dad.

'I can't because it's on a really small digital channel and they don't do their programmes on iPlayer,' I said.

'I'm sure it will be repeated,' said Dad.

'Not for ages,' I insisted. 'And I need to know about flesh-eating maggots for this display we're doing at school …'

'Aunt Dora is coming to stay with us,' said Dad.

That shut me up. Whenever people come and stay with us it usually means I have to go and sleep in the attic so they can have my room. I think this is really unfair because I keep all my precious things in my room, namely my collection of Science specimens, and Mum and Dad insist I take them away when people come to stay.

'People don't want to be in a room which is full of jars with vomit and nose pickings and suchlike in,' Mum says.

'But it's Science!' I protest. 'They are specimens of human biology!'

The end result is always the same. I have to lug all my stuff up to the attic and sleep there.

'When's she coming?' I asked.

Dad looked at his watch, and my heart gave a lurch of panic.

'She'll be here in about an hour,' he said, and gave an apologetic sigh. 'I'm sorry, Dave, but there's nowhere else she can stay. Her life has fallen apart.'

'Leaving Uncle Pete is no answer,' I countered. 'Maybe if they went to see a marriage guidance counsellor ...'

'Dora says Pete has fallen in love with someone else.'

'Then why doesn't Pete leave, so Aunt Dora can stay in their house?'

'Dora says she can't stay another moment in that

house because of the pain she's endured in it,' he said. He gave another heavy sigh and repeated: 'I'm sorry, Dave. You're going to have to go up to the attic. And you'll have to clear your stuff out of your room. You know what Dora's like about anything … yukky.'

'My room isn't yukky!' I defended.

'The things in it are,' said Dad.

'Why can't Aunt Dora go in Krystal's room?' I asked.

Even as I said it I knew it was a lost cause. Krystal is the most terrifying person on the planet, after my gran, but ahead of Banger Bates's dad, and anyone suggesting to her that she give up her room for Aunt Dora would be taking their life in their hands.

'You need to get your stuff moved, Dave,' said Dad.

'But—' I began.

Then I shut up and just gave a heavy sigh. I was beaten and I knew it. 'Can I watch the end of this programme first?' I asked.

Dad hesitated, then nodded. 'All right,' he said.

I grabbed the remote and switched the TV back on, but the programme about the flesh-eating maggots had ended. Instead there was something on about the best colour wallpaper to decorate your living room with. I switched the TV off.

'She won't be here for long, Dave,' said Dad. 'And she is my sister.'

CHAPTER 3

I went upstairs to my room with a heavy heart. Fred came padding up the stairs behind me. He could tell I was unhappy, and he wagged his tail to try and cheer me up. It was lucky for me he did wag his tail, because he let off a juicy fart and his tail fanned the smell down towards Dad, who staggered back, clutching his throat and nose.

'And that dog stays outside while Dora's here!' choked Dad, pointing an angry finger at Fred.

I didn't reply.

Inside my room, I looked around at my precious Science collection: my microscope and all the slides neatly packed into separate boxes, and the other boxes with different specimens in, and felt sad. Didn't Dad realise how fragile so much of this stuff was? Moving it could damage some of the samples. For example, dried vomit on a tissue forms a crusty layer which can crack and fall apart and just turn into dust.

Luckily I wouldn't have to move my computer. I was pretty sure that even someone as mad as Aunt Dora wouldn't be afraid of a laptop. As I looked at my laptop, I remembered the TV programme I'd been watching, and how it had been interrupted at a crucial and exciting moment. If I could find out who had made the programme, maybe I could email them and ask them to send me a copy of it. Or even find out if I could download it.

While Fred went sniffing around my room for

interesting smells, I started to search, and soon found out which company had made the programme I'd been watching. They had a 'contact us' link on their website, so I sent them an email with my name and address and asked if they could either let me download the programme, or send me a DVD of it.

I'd just finished doing that when I heard raised voices from downstairs. It was Dad and Mum arguing. Mum had obviously just returned home from her evening class and Dad had told her the

news about Aunt Dora coming to stay. She was clearly not pleased. I went to my door and opened it so I could hear better.

'Why on earth did you agree she could come and stay?' demanded Mum.

'Because she's my sister and there's nowhere else she can go,' defended Dad.

'But she's awful,' said Mum. 'She weeps all over the place when she's in a good mood! And she's neurotic.'

'She's always been a bit nervous,' admitted Dad.

'A *bit*?! She has enough phobias to keep a whole continent of psychiatrists in work! She's afraid of

FACTOID:
Phobias
As well as well-known phobias like claustrophobia (fear of confined spaces) and altophobia (fear of flying) there are also more unusual ones ones such as chorophobia (fear of dancing) and ablutophobia (fear of washing or cleaning).

loud noises, quiet noises, heights, dogs, cats, birds, horses …'

'She had a bad experience once with a horse,' said Dad. 'It trod on her foot.'

'Someone once knocked me down on their bike but I don't have a fit of the terrors whenever I see a bicycle!' said Mum.

'I'm sorry,' said Dad, 'but when she asked I couldn't say no. She is my sister.'

Frankly, that had seemed a pretty poor argument when Dad had said it to me. Krystal's my sister, but if she phoned me up wanting to come and move in when we were older, I'd say 'No!' very firmly. Providing she didn't ask me face to face, that is, but only on the phone from somewhere a very long way away, because otherwise she'd just bash me and move in anyway.

I decided to put packing up my stuff on hold for a while, because it seemed that Mum also didn't fancy the idea of Aunt Dora coming to stay with us. And as Mum usually won any arguments she had with Dad, there was a good chance I'd get to stay in my room after all.

But, in this case, instead of Mum saying 'So what?' to Dad's comment about Aunt Dora being his sister, she sighed sympathetically and said, 'Yes, I suppose you're right. Families have to look after each other.'

I turned and looked at Fred.

'Well, that's it, Fred,' I said gloomily. 'I'm going to have to move up to the attic after all. And you're going to spend most of the time in your kennel.'

Suddenly the door to my bedroom opened even wider and Mum looked in.

'Ah, good,' she said. 'You're packing up your stuff. Don't be long about it. Dora will be here soon and I need to change the sheets on your bed.' She cast a doubtful look at Fred. 'And make sure that dog doesn't make any bad smells in here. I don't want to give Dora anything to complain about.'

'Right, Mum,' I said.

With that, she went, obviously to clean the house

from top to bottom in readiness for Aunt Dora's visit.

I looked at Fred.

'Go on, Fred,' I appealed to him. 'Just one last one. Then maybe she won't be able to stay here.'

Fred looked at me and wagged his tail. I could swear he even smiled. And then he farted. I held my nose and smiled back at him.

'Good boy, Fred,' I said.

CHAPTER 4

I moved all my stuff up to the attic and made up the old rickety camp bed there. And then I put Fred in his kennel. I was just about to go back indoors when Krystal arrived home from Shelly's. She saw me putting Fred in his kennel and said: 'Good. Mum's made you kick him out of the house. About time too. That dog smells the place up. I can't bring my friends back home because of him.'

'Aunt Dora's coming to stay,' I said gloomily.

Her reaction was immediate. She grabbed me by the hair in a grip of iron, hauled me painfully off the ground, and glared at me.

'What have you done?!' she hissed.

'Aaaarghh!' I yelled, as my hair began to pop out by the roots. 'It wasn't my fault!'

Fred growled and bared his teeth at Krystal, and Mum came out to see what all the noise was about.

'Krystal, stop playing with Dave,' she said.

Playing? My sister was tearing my hair out in lumps and Mum called it 'playing'!

'We have to get the house ready for your Aunt Dora,' added Mum. 'She'll be here in about ten minutes.'

Krystal gaped at her, in a state of shock. 'Why's she coming here?' she demanded angrily.

'Her marriage has broken up and she needs somewhere to stay as a sanctuary while she recovers,' said Mum.

'Africa,' said Krystal. 'They have sanctuaries there. We did them in school.'

'Dora is in need of our help,' began Mum, and I took the opportunity to sneak off and head upstairs to the attic. I'd already heard as much as I needed to know about Aunt Dora and Uncle Pete's broken marriage.

I spent the next half hour making sure my collection of Science specimens was stored safely in the attic, and that there weren't any holes in the roof. I'm convinced that animals live in our attic: birds and mice and other small furry animals that find their way in through holes and things. I've never seen them, but I've heard them.

FACTOID:
Rat Fleas
People think that rats caused the worst plagues in history, but these plagues were actually spread by the fleas that lived on rats. When the rats died, the fleas jumped on to humans. Fleas have an internal thermometer that tells them when a rat is about to die, so they can leave the rat.

Aunt Dora didn't arrive for another hour. That's another thing about Aunt Dora, she's always late, because she has these phobias about having left the doors unlocked, or the tap running, or something. I was at her house once when Dad and I were meant to be taking her somewhere. We were all ready to go, and as Dora was about to leave the house and get into our car, she said: 'I'll just check I haven't left the gas on.'

So she went into the kitchen to make sure the gas was turned off (it was). She then went round the house checking that she'd locked all the doors (she had) and that the windows were firmly shut (they were) and that the rubbish had been put out in the dustbin (it had been). After fifteen minutes of this, she almost got into the car, but stopped because she said the air freshener Dad had hanging in the front contained toxic fumes which might kill her, so Dad had to take it off and get rid of it. And she wouldn't allow him to just throw it in her dustbin, he had to wrap it up 'for security' first.

That's why Aunt Dora is always late. It's a shame, really, and I suppose she can't help it, but it is very irritating when you're waiting for her.

I knew that she'd finally arrived when I heard

Mum shouting up the stairs at me: 'Dave! Come down and say hello to your Aunt Dora!'

When I got downstairs, Aunt Dora was standing there with the usual suspects: Mum, Dad and Krystal. Mum and Dad had those fixed smiles on their faces that people wear when they try to cheer someone up. Krystal just scowled.

'Say hello to your Aunt Dora,' Mum repeated, with forced cheerfulness.

'Hello, Aunt Dora,' I said, and I held out my hand to shake hers. I have found this to be a good ploy with female relatives, otherwise they tend to grab you and plant wet kisses on the top of your head. One way to stop them doing that is to tell them you've got head lice, but I knew that would only

FACTOID:
Head Lice
Lice live on warm human skin and suck blood. Female head lice glue their eggs – called nits – to human hair.

start Aunt Dora quivering and get me into trouble with Mum and Dad.

Aunt Dora looked at my hand suspiciously, as if inspecting it for germs, and then swayed and burst into tears.

'I'm sorry,' she blubbed, 'but Dave looks so like Pete and it just reminds me of the pain he's caused me.'

This baffled me. How on earth could I look

anything like her husband when I wasn't related to him genetically? However, it seemed like a good excuse to get out of talking to her, so I put on my Looking Sad face and said: 'I'm very sorry, Aunt Dora. I'll do my best to stay out of your way while you're here.'

Krystal realised what I was doing and glared at me so fiercely I thought she was going to tear my liver out and eat it. I decided it would be good timing to nip back upstairs to the attic while I was ahead of the game, but then my luck ran out. Dora stopped weeping long enough to moan: 'No, no, it's something I have to learn to live with. Perhaps the more I see of you, the better it will help me cope with my pain.'

At this, Krystal smirked. My heart sank. It was bad enough having Aunt Dora living with us and casting a cloud over the whole house, but now I was going to have to spend time with her so she could keep looking at me.

Just then we heard Fred barking from outside,

which made Aunt Dora jump and start shaking. I grabbed the opportunity.

'I'd better take Fred for his evening walk,' I said. 'He needs to do a poo.'

The mention of the word 'poo' made Aunt Dora look a bit queasy, so I just smiled politely, grabbed Fred's lead, and headed off.

While Aunt Dora was with us, Fred was going to be getting lots of walks.

CHAPTER 5

Next morning I called for my best friend, Paul, so we could walk to school together. I wanted to tell him about Aunt Dora coming to stay and how unfair it was that I had been stuck in the attic once again. Unfortunately, all Paul wanted to talk about was this model he was making of the universe for our Science Display.

'I've made it out of these different-sized balls,' he said. 'I've got a tennis ball for the Earth, with a golf ball for the moon—'

'That's not going to work,' I pointed out. 'The sun is so much bigger than the Earth, and so are some of the outer planets. You won't be able to get a ball big enough.'

'I have already,' he said. 'I've got a football for

Saturn and a balloon for the sun. And they're all going to hang from string.'

'It won't be as good as my model of the human brain,' I said.

'Yes, it will,' said Paul. 'My model moves. All the planets will spin.'

That shut me up. I had to admit, Paul's model would be pretty impressive with everything moving.

FACTOID:
Our Solar System
The planets in our solar system are: Mercury, Venus, Earth, Mars, Jupiter, Saturn, Uranus and Neptune. They all go round the sun. Mercury is the smallest, and Jupiter is the biggest.

'I wonder if I can make my brain do something interesting?' I said. 'Maybe I can make it move around. At the moment it just lies there and wobbles.'

'Then it might look like one of those monsters you see in sci-fi movies,' Paul pointed out.

'Good point,' I agreed.

I was still pondering interesting features for my human brain when I was hit behind by something like a cross between a fast-moving rottweiler and a tank.

'Ow!' I cried out, as I crashed to the pavement.

'Anwar!' yelled an angry voice.

It was our classmate and friend, Sukijeet Patel. I sat up on the pavement and looked round. Suki's six-year-old brother, Anwar, was also sitting up near me, holding his head.

'Ow!' he said.

Suki came hurrying over and hauled him to his feet.

'You are terrible, Anwar!' she told him crossly. 'You could have torn your clothes.'

'He might have broken my leg,' I pointed out.

'Sorry,' said Anwar, rubbing his head. 'I was playing at being a racing car.'

Suki took Anwar firmly by the collar of his jacket to make sure he didn't go running off, and joined us as we carried on walking to school.

'I saw a fantastic programme on TV last night about insects in Africa that lay their eggs in people's wounds, and their maggots eat their way through the people's flesh,' I told her.

'Ugh, gross!' said Paul.

'Yes, I know about them,' said Suki. 'I think they're called screw-worms.' Then she added, 'Do you know in this country they sometimes use maggots on patients in hospital? The maggots eat the rotten flesh around the patient's wound ...'

FACTOID:
Maggots
Maggots are often used to treat infected wounds. They eat the infected skin around the wound, leaving it clean and stopping the infection spreading.

'Oh double gross!' complained Paul.

'On this programme they had maggots popping out from the back of a man's neck,' I told Suki.

'My model of the universe moves!' said Paul, firmly and proudly.

'People will be impressed by my model of the human brain,' I repeated, drawn straight back into the argument we were having before Anwar knocked me over.

'No one's going to bother with your brain when they can see a model of the universe that actually moves,' Paul declared.

I had a feeling he might be right.

When we got to school I was surprised to see our class teacher, Miss Moore, and our head teacher, Miss Nelson, standing at the school gates with very grim expressions.

'They look like they're waiting for someone,' murmured Suki.

'And that someone is going to be in trouble, by the look of their faces,' added Paul.

I was just about to add: 'I wonder who that someone is?' when Miss Nelson pointed at me. 'Dave Dickens,' she said sternly. 'We want to talk to you!'

'Dave's in trouble!' chuckled Anwar, but then Suki grabbed him by the arm and hissed at him to shut up, and rushed him into the playground. Paul gave me a sympathetic look and mouthed, 'I'll see you later' before hurrying after her.

I was bewildered. What had I done wrong? Nothing.

Miss Nelson gestured for me to move to one corner of the playground, and I followed her, with Miss Moore traipsing after us. Then they turned on me with glowering faces, like those nasty interrogators you see in war films.

'Dave, was it you who put a pretend brain in the fridge in the kitchens?' demanded Miss Nelson.

'It's not a pretend brain,' I said. 'It's a *model* brain. For the Science Display our class are doing. Aren't we, Miss Moore?'

Miss Nelson shot a hard look at Miss Moore when she heard this, and asked, 'Well, Miss Moore?'

Miss Moore groaned. 'Yes, it's true Dave is making a model of the brain for our display, but I didn't know he'd put it in the fridge.' Then she turned to me and said, 'Did you ask me for permission to put it in the fridge in the kitchens?'

'No,' I admitted. 'But when I saw it was starting to melt I knew I had to put it somewhere cold. I couldn't take it home because it would have melted by the time I got there, or I might have dropped it as I walked, because it wobbles.'

FACTOID:
Gelatin

Gelatin is a transparent jelly-like substance used in making jellies and medicine capsules. It is made from animal skin and bones that are melted down. The collagen that comes out in the process is collected to make gelatin.

'Quiet!' snapped Miss Nelson.

'I did put a note on it saying what it was,' I pointed out.

'Exactly,' growled Miss Nelson. 'And when Mrs Worple opened the door of the kitchen fridge first thing this morning and saw a wobbly pink brain on a plate with a note on it saying "Dave Dickens' Brain" …'

Suddenly I realised why they were angry. Poor Mrs Worple must have had a shock when she saw that. But it wasn't my fault! I was only making sure my model brain was in good condition for our Science Display. And the note I'd put on it was meant to be helpful.

'Was Mrs Worple upset?' I asked, doing my best to look very sorry.

'Mrs Worple has had to go home with a severe case of shock,' snapped Miss Nelson. 'I believe she will be off work for at least a week with severe Post-Traumatic Stress.'

'Oh dear,' I said, trying to look even more sorry.

'Shall I go and see her and apologise?'

Miss Nelson and Miss Moore looked at one another, and then Miss Nelson said, 'No, I don't think that's a good idea. The thought that someone had removed your brain and put it on a plate in her fridge is still too fresh in her mind. Seeing you might trigger an unfortunate recurrence. Just make sure you never do anything like that again.'

'I won't,' I promised.

'In the meantime, I suppose you'd better leave your model brain in the fridge to make sure it doesn't melt.'

'Yes, Miss Nelson,' I said. 'Thank you, Miss Nelson.'

Miss Nelson then looked at Miss Moore and said sniffily, 'We shall discuss this later, Miss Moore.' So I knew that I wasn't the only one in trouble.

CHAPTER 6

Apart from that, the rest of the day was pretty normal. Nothing much of interest happened. We did Literacy and Numeracy in the morning, and then in the afternoon we did Art. Paul did a painting of Space, I did a diagram of a human brain to go with my wobbly model, Suki made this clever diagram of how a fly's eyes work, and Banger Bates, the school bully, was supposed to be making a collage, but he tried sniffing the glue off a brush and the brush got stuck up the inside of his nostril.

When I got home Aunt Dora was in the kitchen crying to Mum about how she'd given the best years of her life to Pete and now he'd just thrown here away like an old shoe, so I took Fred for a walk.

When I got home Dora was still in the kitchen crying, but by now Dad had arrived home and it was his turn to listen to her.

I was just heading up to my attic, when Krystal appeared from the living room and grabbed me.

'Mum says we have to talk to Aunt Dora and entertain her and keep her mind off things,' she hissed menacingly. 'So that means you. I'm going round to Shelly's.'

With that Krystal nipped off. As she was taking her school bag with her, I guessed she wouldn't be back until bed-time.

I was just standing there, wondering what I could talk to Aunt Dora about, when Mum appeared.

'Ah, Dave,' she said. 'Did Krystal talk to you?'

'Yes,' I said.

'Good,' she said. 'Go and talk to your aunt. Cheer her up.' With that she called out: 'John! I need your help!'

Dad appeared from the kitchen with a grateful look of relief on his face. 'Yes?' he asked.

'Dave says he'll chat to Aunt Dora,' said Mum.

And with that she gave me a push in the back and I found myself in the kitchen. Aunt Dora looked up at me, wiping the tears from her eyes.

'Dave!' she said. 'There's no need for you to spend your time with unhappy me!'

'OK,' I said, and I headed out of the kitchen.

I didn't get far. Mum grabbed me before I got to the stairs.

'Get back in there and cheer her up!' she hissed, with almost as much menace as Krystal. I guess the ability to be terrifying runs in the women in our family.

'Right,' I sighed, and I wandered back into the kitchen.

'That's all right, Aunt Dora,' I said. 'I'd like to keep you company and cheer you up. Take your mind off things.'

'Ten years!' she announced suddenly, and for a horrible moment I thought she was saying that's how long she intended to stay with us.

'What?' I asked.

'Pete and I were married for ten years!' she said. 'And now he's just thrown it away for some woman dentist!'

'Oh dear,' I said sympathetically.

Aunt Dora lapsed into a moody silence, sitting at the kitchen table, staring at nothing. I thought this might be a good time to sneak off, but I knew I'd never get past Mum.

'Entertain her,' Mum had said. 'Take her mind off things.'

I racked my brain for something to say that might cheer her up. Then I remembered what our teacher, Miss Moore, had told us when we all had to do a talk in front of the class:

'Your talk will be more entertaining if you talk about something you enjoy doing or are interested in.'

'Did you know that when someone sneezes, the snot comes out of their nose at a hundred and sixty kilometres an hour?' I said.

Aunt Dora looked at me, stunned. 'What?' she said.

'Did you know that the acids in your stomach are so powerful they can dissolve metal?' I added brightly.

'Dave!' called Mum threateningly from outside. 'Can I have a word with you?'

Next morning I got up early so I could eat breakfast
without having Aunt Dora crying at me. Fortunately,
she didn't seem to get up before half past eight. I was
just passing the front door when the doorbell rang.
It was the postman with a small packet.

'Here you are,' he said.

It was addressed to DJ Dickens, which is me, and
was from some company called Transit Materials,
which was a name I didn't recognise. Then it
suddenly struck me that it might be the DVD of
the programme about the flesh-eating maggots!
The packet looked about the right sort of size and
shape.

I opened the packet. There was a small flat plastic

box inside it. I took it out, and was puzzled to see that something seemed to be moving under the transparent lid. Then I realised there were a whole *load* of things moving. I looked closer, and realised with a shock they were maggots! Instead of just sending me a DVD of the programme, they'd sent me a box filled with flesh-eating maggots!

CHAPTER 7

To say I was shocked was an understatement. Here I was holding a plastic box filled with flesh-eating maggots! If the lid of the box had come off even just a bit, the maggots would have been all over me and started munching their way through me!

Quickly I pushed the plastic box back inside the packet, and then stuffed that in my school bag.

What could I do? I couldn't just throw them away because they would crawl along until they found someone and ate them. If I told Dad and Mum, it would cause a panic in the house and I'd get the blame and get told off. The only thing to do was keep them sealed tightly inside the plastic container and take them to school with me, where at least

I could keep an eye on them while I worked out what to do.

When I got to school Paul was already in the playground blowing up a blue balloon.

'What's that for?' I asked.

'This is the sun for my project.'

'It's blue,' I pointed out. 'The sun is red.'

FACTOID:
The Sun
The sun is so big it makes up 99.86% of the mass of our solar system.

'I couldn't find a red balloon big enough,' he replied. And he started blowing it up even more.

'Stop!' I said. 'I've got something terrible to tell you!'

Paul gave one last puff into his balloon, and it burst with a loud bang.

'Ow!' he said. He gazed at the shrivelled piece of blue rubber in his hand and then looked at me accusingly. 'What did you do to my balloon?' he demanded.

'I didn't do anything!' I protested. 'It just went bang. You blew too much air into it. Anyway, I've got to tell you about the maggots.'

'What maggots?' he asked.

'The ones I was telling you and Suki about yesterday,' I said. 'The ones that eat into people's flesh.'

'Oh gross!' he said, pulling a face.

I patted my school bag. 'Well I've got some.'

Paul looked at me, stunned. 'You've what?' he asked.

'I've got some of those maggots in here.'

Paul began moving back. 'Stay away from me!' he ordered.

'No, it's all right, they're in a plastic container,' I said.

'If they can eat through a body, surely they can eat through plastic,' he said.

I must admit that was something that I hadn't

thought of before. I took a quick look at the packet, and at the plastic box inside it, but everything seemed to be secure.

'No, they're OK,' I said.

'How did you get hold of them?' demanded Paul.

I noticed he was still standing about five metres away from me, which meant he had to shout so I could hear him.

'Don't shout!' I said. 'Everyone will hear. Come nearer so we can talk.'

'Not likely,' said Paul.

'They're safe,' I assured him. 'The television company sent them to me, so they must know what they're doing.'

Still not looking entirely convinced, Paul edged a bit nearer. 'Why did they send them to you?' he asked.

'It was a mistake,' I said. And I told him about how I'd emailed the company asking for a DVD of the programme, and instead they'd sent me a packet of the actual maggots.

'Well I'm not sitting in the same class as you if you've got those in your bag,' he said. 'They might escape and start eating me.'

'They won't escape,' I said.

'They might,' he said. 'It was in this film I saw: *Curse of the Maggot People*. These maggots came from outer space and invaded Earth and began eating their way into people's brains and controlling them.'

'This is not a film, this is real life!' I protested.

'I'm still not sitting in the same room as those maggots,' he insisted.

'Well what can I do with them?' I demanded. 'I can't throw them away.'

'Put them in your locker,' said Paul.

I thought it over. 'I don't know,' I said doubtfully.

'They'll be as safe in your locker as in your bag,' said Paul. 'At least the packet won't get swung about like it would if it was in your bag.'

'OK,' I said. 'But we've got to work out what to do about them.'

'Ask Suki,' suggested Paul. 'She knows about insects.'

I didn't get the chance to ask Suki about the maggots until breaktime, because she was late. Her terrible little brother, Anwar, had got his head stuck in the railings of a fence on his way to school.

When we told her, her mouth dropped open in shock.

'You can't keep them here!' she said.

'Well I can't keep them at home,' I said. 'Dad and Mum would go mad if they knew about them.'

'You have to take them to the police,' she said firmly. 'Or the local Health Office. They'll know what to do.'

'Won't I get into trouble?' I asked.

'No,' Suki said. 'In fact you'll be a hero for handing them in.'

Being called a hero sounded quite good, so I decided I'd take them to the Health Office, or the police, at lunchtime. That way I wouldn't have to explain to Mum and Dad why I was late home from school.

As soon as the bell went for lunchtime, I hurried to my locker and opened it.

The packet of maggots was gone.

CHAPTER 8

'Aaaargh!!' I went.

Paul was opening his own locker near me. When he heard me yell, he leapt about four metres in the air and started panicking.

'Have they escaped!' he asked, looking terrified, his eyes darting around the floor and walls looking for writhing maggots.

'Yes and no,' I said. 'The whole packet's gone! Someone's taken it!'

Paul stopped looking nervous, and instead looked puzzled. 'Are you sure?' he asked.

'See for yourself,' I said, and I showed him my empty locker.

Paul shook his head and kept well away from my locker, just in case there were escaped maggots lurking in wait for him. But then he peered towards it. 'The parcel's gone as well,' he said.

'Exactly,' I nodded. 'Like I said, someone's taken it.'

'But who'd want to take a packet of flesh-eating maggots?' Paul asked. 'I mean, who even knew they were there?'

'Everyone who heard you shouting about them in the playground this morning,' I said grumpily.

'I wasn't shouting,' Paul defended. Then a thought struck him. 'Banger Bates!'

'What?' I asked.

'When we were talking about the maggots and putting them in your locker, Banger Bates was just walking past. And he went rushing out of our classroom when the bell went just now for lunch.'

'Why would Banger Bates want to steal flesh-eating maggots?' I asked. 'You'd have to be stupid to want to do that.'

'Exactly,' nodded Paul. 'And who's the most stupid person we know?'

Paul had a good point. Banger Bates has the biggest fists I've ever seen – apart from his dad's – and he is enormous. In fact he is so big I'm not sure he should be in our school, or our class. He looks like he's fifteen or something. But he is really stupid.

I still couldn't work out what Banger Bates would do with a packet of flesh-eating maggots. Maybe there was someone he wanted to be eaten by them. Or maybe he was going to use them as a weapon, to threaten someone with.

'I'd better find him,' I said. 'If those maggots escape …'

'They could eat the whole town,' finished Paul. 'Just like happened in that film, *Curse of the Maggot People.*'

As I rushed out into the playground, one side of me was saying: 'Leave Banger Bates alone. He'll beat you up. And with a bit of luck the maggots will eat him.' But another side of me was worried about all the other kids at school who might get eaten as well.

As it turned out, Banger Bates wasn't around. Someone had seen him nip out of school as soon as lunchtime started. All I could do was hang around and wait for him to come back. I asked Paul if he'd wait with me, but Paul said he needed to find another balloon for his project after he'd eaten his sandwiches.

I spent the next twenty minutes waiting by the school gates. One of the dinner ladies on playground duty came and asked me if I was all right, because she said I looked ill. I told her I was fine, but she didn't look convinced, so I put on a big smile to prove it. The trouble was she didn't believe me, and although she wandered off, she kept throwing looks at me. Every time she did I had to put my Big Smile on, and by the time twenty minutes had past my face had got stuck into this Big Smile and was aching. So when Banger Bates turned up and I ran towards him, he scowled and demanded aggressively: 'What you laughing at?'

'Nothing,' I said quickly. 'I've got toothache and this is the only thing that stops it hurting.'

'Idiot!' he snapped, and he walked past, knocking me aside.

I hurried after him. 'Did you find a packet of maggots?' I asked him urgently.

'No,' he grunted, glaring at me.

I knew he was lying. Actually, Banger always lies. I don't know why, because telling the truth would be simpler, and for someone as thick as Banger it would mean he wouldn't have to try and remember the last lie he told.

'Anyway, what would I want with your maggots?' he sneered.

'How did you know they were mine?' I asked.

Banger frowned at that, and I could almost see his poor one brain cell trying to come up with a clever answer. When it failed, he reached out and grabbed me by the shirt and lifted me off the ground.

'I'm gonna beat you up!' he snarled, and he drew back his fist.

'Those maggots eat people!' I said desperately.

This sentence stopped Banger in his tracks. He looked at me, his big fist poised ready to strike, my feet dangling just above the ground.

'What?' he said.

'Those maggots aren't just ordinary maggots,' I said. 'They are flesh-eating maggots from Africa. They got sent to me by mistake. They burrow into people's skin and get inside their bodies and then eat their way out.'

Banger let go of my shirt and I dropped back to the ground. He looked sick.

'I gave them to my dad as bait for going fishing this afternoon,' he croaked hoarsely.

'If he opens the packet, they'll kill him,' I said. 'They'll eat him. They'll start by finding a hole somewhere, his nostrils or his ear, and they'll burrow their way inside his body and eat their way out.'

Banger staggered backwards. For a second I thought he was going to faint. 'We gotta get 'em back!' he said.

'We?' I said. 'You were the one who gave them to

your dad. *You'd* better go and get them back.'

'I can't!' he said, anguished. 'I told him I'd bought 'em as a present. If I tell him what they really are, he'll kill me!'

'If you don't, they'll kill *him*,' I pointed out.

Suddenly he grabbed me by the collar with one of his enormous hands. 'This is all your fault!' he snarled. 'If you hadn't brung 'em into school ...'

'You stole them!' I protested.

'*You're* gonna get 'em back off my dad!' he screamed.

'No I'm not!' I said.

I was scared of Banger, but I was even more scared of his dad. Banger's dad is one of these men with more tattoos on them than they've actually got skin. And he has these eyes that look like a serial killer's.

'Yes you are!' grated Banger.

'I don't know where your dad is!' I said.

'He's at the canal,' said Banger.

'But I don't know *where*,' I pointed out. 'The canal is miles long.'

'I know where he fishes,' said Banger. His grip on my collar tightened. 'I'll take you.'

CHAPTER 9

As Banger Bates dragged me along the street by my collar, I kept thinking that I was now a truant, even if it wasn't my fault. I sort of half-walked and was half-dragged along by the ever more frantic Banger, who kept repeating all the time: 'What are we going to tell him? What are we going to tell him?' in a nervous voice that showed he wasn't looking forward to telling his dad he couldn't use the maggots.

'Maybe we won't have to say anything,' I said. 'Maybe the maggots will have eaten him.'

Bash! Banger thumped me in the ear with his free fist. 'Don't you say that sort of thing about my dad!' he growled.

We hurried along through the streets like this for about a mile. No one stopped us! It must have been obvious to all the passers-by that I was being kidnapped, but no one stepped in and tried to save me. To be fair, if I'd been a passer-by and taken a look at Banger, I don't think I'd have tried to interfere either. He may not have been bright, but he looked like a big thug.

By the time we got to the towpath of the canal I was out of breath and half-strangled by my collar, which was now so far up around my head I was having to look through the buttonholes of my shirt to see where we were going.

'There he is!' said Banger, and he stopped suddenly and I crashed into him and fell over.

'Ow!' I said.

Banger wasn't listening to me. He was looking along the towpath to where his dad was standing, preparing his fishing gear. He looked terrified. I'd seen Banger look like this before, but that had also been when he was with his dad and his dad was telling him off. I suppose this is what these psychologists and psychiatrists mean when they say that 'bullies are to be pitied because they are people who have been bullied'. But, to be honest, I don't pity Banger at all. He's too mean and scary for that.

'What are we going to tell him?' said Banger in a frightened whisper for about the zillionth time.

Now I wasn't being bounced up and down along the road, I could think.

'We tell him the maggots have got a disease,' I suggested. 'And if he uses them they'll kill the fish.'

Banger looked at me, his mouth dropping open, and for a second I thought he was going to sneer 'Stupid!' like he usually does and bash me. But instead he said: 'Brilliant! You tell him!'

'Why me?' I started to say, but I'd only got the first word out when I felt myself being lifted off the ground again by my shirt and dragged along the towpath by Banger. Once again my shirt came up and covered my face so I couldn't see properly.

'Dad!' he yelled. 'Don't use those maggots!'

I managed to get a look at Banger's dad through

my buttonhole. He was standing looking at us with a puzzled expression on his face. Or again, it could just have been one of his many tattoos.

'What?' he said.

Banger put me down. Now I could see that Mr Bates was holding the plastic container with the maggots in and was just about to open it.

'Don't open those maggots!' said Banger desperately.

'Why not?' asked Mr Bates, looking bewildered.

Banger pushed me forward. 'Dickens here will tell you,' he said.

Mr Bates looked at me. 'I know you,' he said. 'You're the boy who looks after my mum's dog.'

'That's right,' I swallowed.

'How is he?'

'Very well,' I said cautiously.

'Is he still farting?' he asked, and he laughed.

Banger's dad laughing was an even more terrifying sound than a rottweiler growling. It was this low rumble that came up from somewhere

inside his enormous frame, and when he opened his lips to let it out you could see all the gold fillings in his teeth. He must have had a whole bank's worth of money in his mouth.

'Now and then,' I said. 'But they're not as smelly as they used to be. Most of the time.'

'The maggots!' hissed Banger urgently in my ear.

'Yeh,' said Mr Bates. 'What about 'em?'

'They've got a disease,' I said. 'They might kill the fish.'

Mr Bates frowned. 'What sort of disease?'

I hadn't expected him to ask that. Desperately I tried to think of the name of a disease that affected maggots, but I couldn't. I'm OK when it comes to human diseases because my hobby is human biology and that's what I want to do when I leave school, but insects are Suki's department.

'Er …' I said.

'Let's see what's wrong with 'em,' said Mr Bates, and with that he pulled the lid off the container.

'No!' yelled Banger in alarm. He leapt forward to

FACTOID:
Fish Diseases

Many fish suffer illnesses from parasites that latch on to their scales. Often other smaller fish known as 'cleaner fish' will clean and eat the parasites off a larger fish.

try and push the lid back on, but he tripped and fell and knocked the container out of his dad's hands. The maggots flew up in the air and then landed on Banger, in his hair and on his clothes.

'AAAARGHHH!!!' screamed Banger. 'They're eating me!'

In desperation he hurled himself into the canal, right under the water. Luckily the canal is only about four feet deep, so when he stood up, dripping wet, his head and shoulders were sticking out of the water.

Mr Bates stared at him, stunned. 'Edward!'

I decided I didn't want to be there for the explanations, and anyway the maggots were now out in the open, so I turned and headed off back along the towpath as fast as I could. Behind me I could hear splashing sounds as Banger fell over, and stood up again, and bashed at the water with his hands to stop the maggots getting on to him, but I didn't hang around to find out what happened next. Escape was my only plan.

CHAPTER 10

By the time I got back to school it was half past two, only half an hour to go before the bell for home time. I wondered how to get back in without being seen. And I wondered if Miss Moore, our class teacher, had noticed that I wasn't in her classroom. It's amazing with teachers. Sometimes they act as if you're invisible – usually when you know the answer to something for once – and other times when you secretly do something like stick your finger up your nose to pick a bogie out they shout: 'Dave Dickens! Take your finger out of your nose!'

School, like life, can be very unfair.

Luckily I couldn't see anyone about. I decided that what I would do was sneak into the toilets, and then come out and tell Miss Moore that I'd been stuck in the toilet all afternoon with a serious case of diarrhoea.

I was just heading across the playground towards the main building, when I heard a voice call out: 'Dave Dickens! Come here!'

It was Miss Moore.

I walked towards her as slowly as I could, desperately trying to come up with some plausible excuses about where I'd been. Could I say I'd fainted and had only just recovered consciousness? That might work. Or that I'd been sent on an errand by another teacher and got lost? But then she'd ask me which other teacher had sent me on the errand.

FACTOID:
Fainting
Fainting is a temporary loss of consciousness caused by not enough oxygen in the brain. The causes can include low blood pressure, standing up too quickly or being in a very hot room.

I decided to use the fainting excuse, and was just trying to remember whether it was low blood pressure or high blood pressure that caused it when Miss Moore said: 'You have been truanting!'

'No!' I protested. 'What happened was …'

'You were seen sneaking off with Edward Bates,' she said. She sighed and gave a sad shake of her head. 'I will have to tell your parents, Dave.'

'What?!' I said, shocked. 'No!'

'Yes,' she said. 'I don't want to, but these things have to be nipped in the bud or they get worse. I have always considered you one of the more able children in my class, Dave, and I have high hopes for you. But the danger is that when boys reach your age, they can become rebellious.'

'I'm not rebellious,' I protested.

'Not yet,' she said. 'That's because I've spotted it before it has got to that stage. Do you want to be a hoodie, Dave?'

'No,' I said.

'Exactly,' she said.

'But it was only for an hour!' I protested.

'An hour and a half,' she said.

'And I wasn't doing anything bad!'

'Then what were you doing?' she asked.

At this I fell silent. Confessing would mean telling her about the flesh-eating maggots, and that Banger had stolen them from me to give to his dad. And, if I told her that, Banger would bash me up for squealing on him.

I looked at her with what I hoped was an appealing smile, a plea for leniency. Another chance for a First Time Offender.

Miss Moore gave a heavy sigh. 'We have to stop this before it gets worse, Dave,' she said. 'Today it's an hour and a half. Next time it will be a whole day, and then it will be a week, and you'll fail your education and end up spending a wasted life, unable to get a decent job. It is my duty as your teacher to see that doesn't happen to you. Now get to class.'

I trudged towards the main building with a heavy heart. My life was falling to ruins about my ears.

And all because I'd emailed a TV company and asked for a copy of their stupid programme! That was me furthering my education, and what did I get for it? Labelled a rebel and a hoodie! Life was so unfair!

CHAPTER 11

By the time I got back to class, a music lesson with Mrs Armstrong was just ending. That was one good thing. Mrs Armstrong is about as musical as a brick. She's supposed to have been a proper violin player and she comes in now and then to do music with us, but most of the time she sings at us. As she's got a voice that sounds like a chainsaw, it's a nightmare.

As I packed up my things to go home, Paul and Suki rushed over to find out what had happened. I told them about Banger dragging me off to find his dad, and the maggots getting all over him, and him jumping in the canal. And then the really bad news about getting caught by Miss Moore as a truant, and that she would be phoning Mum and Dad to tell them.

'But what happened to the maggots?' asked Suki.

'I told you, they fell in the canal,' I said.

'Well that's one good thing,' said Paul. 'They'll have drowned.'

'Maggots don't drown,' said Suki. 'If they did they wouldn't be any good for fishing with, because the fish see them moving.'

'So they're still alive?' I asked.

'Yes,' said Suki, looking worried. 'And they could spread.'

'What do you mean, "spread"?' I asked nervously.

'They could swim along the canal and wriggle out,' said Suki. She looked at me very seriously. 'You have to report it.'

'I can't,' I protested. 'If I do, I'll get in trouble for taking the maggots to school and Banger Bates will bash me up for telling everyone that he stole them from me.' I turned to Paul and appealed to him. 'You know about maggots.'

'I don't know about maggots,' replied Paul firmly.

'Well you've seen a maggot,' I carried on. 'Do they look the sort of creatures that would go to all the bother of coming out of the water so they could infect people?'

'They did in *Curse of the Maggot People*,' said Paul.

'You said they came from outer space!' I retorted.

'Yes, but their space ship landed in the sea and they swam out and came on land.'

'Salt water would kill maggots,' said Suki.

FACTOID:
Freshwater and Saltwater Fish

Fresh water has a salt level of less than 0.05%. Fish that spend all their lives in fresh water have adapted to this and use their gills to keep the salt inside their bodies. Some fish, such as salmon, live in both fresh and salt water at different times in their lives, and change their bodies to suit the water.

'Ah, but these were alien maggots from another planet,' countered Paul.

'Will you stop going on about these alien maggots!' I shouted. 'They are not real!'

Paul looked at me, upset. 'I'm only trying to help,' he said.

'Well you're not,' I said.

'You have to report these maggots being loose,' repeated Suki. 'It's the proper thing to do.'

I looked at Paul, who nodded. 'Suki's right,' he said.

I let out a deep sigh. 'OK,' I said. 'Who do I tell?'

'The police,' said Suki. 'Now the maggots are out and roaming free, this is an emergency.'

'You have to call 999,' said Paul.

'I know what the number is,' I snapped. Then I sighed again. 'I'm sorry, Paul. I'm a bit jittery at the thought of doing it. I know I'm going to get into even more trouble than I am already.' I swallowed. 'I'll do it anonymously. Can I use your mobile to call them?'

Mum and Dad won't let me have a mobile phone because Mum says the microwaves can damage my brain. That doesn't stop them using their mobiles, and Krystal is on her mobile all the time to her friends.

FACTOID:
Mobile Phones
Mobile phones use electromagnetic radiation. Some scientists believe this can harm human health and have recommended limiting the amount of time people spend on mobile phones.

'No,' said Paul firmly. 'They'll trace the call and it'll come back to me.'

'There's a public pay phone on your way home,' said Suki.

'Right,' I said in a voice of gloom.

'If you don't do the right thing, it always comes back and hurts you later,' said Suki. 'That's what my granddad says.'

'Right,' I said, even more gloomy. 'Will you come with me and give me moral support while I make the call?'

Suki and Paul exchanged awkward looks. Then Paul said: 'We can't. Miss Moore has asked us to help her put up our class's Science Display in the Reception Area after school.'

'That's right,' nodded Suki. 'That's where we're going now.'

I looked at them, shocked. 'But you can't!' I protested. 'What about my brain part of the display? *I* need to do that!'

Paul looked embarrassed. 'I said that to her, but she said that boys who play truant can't be trusted to do things properly,' he said.

'Didn't you tell her I wasn't playing truant?' I demanded.

'I didn't know what you were doing,' said Paul defensively. 'All I knew was you and Banger Bates weren't in school, and that you were waiting for Banger Bates.'

'But …!' I protested angrily.

'It wasn't Paul's fault,' insisted Suki. 'He couldn't cover up for you because he didn't know what was going on.'

I glared at her, then at Paul, and opened my mouth to snap something sarcastic like: 'A fine pair of friends you turned out to be!' But then I didn't say it. The expressions on their faces showed they were unhappy about me being banned from helping do the Science Display. And, as Suki said, it wasn't Paul's fault. Or hers. Suddenly I knew what this was all about. Miss Moore was having her own back on me because she'd got in trouble with Miss Nelson about my brain being found in the kitchen fridge.

'I really wanted to make sure my brain looks good on the display,' I said sadly.

'It will,' Paul assured me. 'We'll make sure of that.'

Then a thought struck me. 'We're supposed to have another couple of days to get things finished. Mrs *Walton's* class are supposed to be doing their display next. They're doing a presentation of cookery and food they've made.'

'I know,' nodded Paul, 'but Health and Safety have told them they can't do it.'

'Why not?' I asked.

'In case anyone eats the food and gets food poisoning. So we've been told our display has to be brought forward.'

Just then, we heard Miss Moore's voice.

'Suki! Paul!' she called. 'Are you coming to help me do the display?'

'Yes, miss,' said Suki. 'I've just got to fetch my brother from Miss Murray's class. He's being kept behind.'

And she hurried off.

Then Paul did a really nice thing. He tried to get Miss Moore to change her mind.

'Miss,' he asked, 'will it be all right if Dave helps us do the display as well? Because he's the only one who knows how to put his model brain out in the display properly.'

I put on a wide friendly smile for Miss Moore. It didn't work. Miss Moore looked at me coldly.

'Dave knows he did wrong today, and wrong-doing shouldn't be rewarded,' she said. 'I'm sorry for Dave, but I hope this way he will learn his lesson.'

And with that she turned and went into our classroom.

Paul gave me an apologetic look. 'I'm sorry,' he said.

'It's not your fault,' I said.

'I'll do my best with your brain,' he promised.

CHAPTER 12

The phone box on my way home wasn't so much an actual box, but a sheet of perspex on a pole with the phone and coin box beneath it. As I approached, I wondered how to go about making the call. Should I pretend to be someone else? Put on some sort of different accent, so they wouldn't know it was me? The trouble is, I'm not very good at accents. I was in a school play once when I had to play the part of Davy Crockett at the Alamo, which was a famous battle in the history of the Wild West of America. I put on my best American Wild West accent, just like the cowboy films I'd seen. Afterwards Mum asked me why I'd played Davy Crockett as Chinese.

I walked backwards and forwards a few times past the phone box, working up the courage to make the call. I was torn between Doing the Right Thing and getting bashed up by Banger. What was so unfair was that none of this was my fault, and I was the one in trouble.

Finally I went to the pay phone and dialled 999. When the operator asked which service I required – Fire, Police or Ambulance – I said: 'All of them.' Then, before she could ask me any more questions, I said: 'There are flesh-eating maggots in the canal near Mertonside Park. They got in there by accident. But if they get out they will eat people.'

Then I hung up and hurried home. And that was when my troubles really began.

FACTOID:
999

999 is the world's oldest emergency call number. It was introduced in the London area in 1937. The number was chosen because '9' was the only number that could be dialled free of charge from the old-fashioned round-dial type phones.

When I arrived home, Fred came bouncing out of his kennel to say hello to me with a smile on his face and his tail wagging. I was just bending down to give him a big hug when I heard Mum's voice.

'Dave. We need to talk to you.'

I looked up. Mum and Dad were both standing at the back door, looking very serious indeed. My heart sank. Miss Moore had obviously phoned them.

I stood up and gave them a big 'Hello, lovely parents!' smile. 'How's Aunt Dora?' I asked, to show them what a kind, thoughtful and caring nephew I was.

'We need to talk,' repeated Mum firmly.

I let Fred go and followed Mum and Dad into the house. Mum had obviously phoned Dad about the situation, which is why he was home early from work.

We went into the kitchen where Krystal was sitting at the table, doing her homework. When she saw me come in she grinned and laughed: 'Here's the bad boy!'

'Krystal, we need to talk to Dave,' said Mum.

'OK,' said Krystal. 'I won't say anything.'

'We need to talk to him *alone*,' added Mum pointedly. 'You can do your homework in your room.'

Krystal opened her mouth as if she was going to protest, then she clamped it shut again. She picked up her school stuff and put it in her bag, and pushed

past me on the way out of the kitchen. My guess was that she would hang around outside so she could hear what was going on.

'Dave,' said Mum. 'Miss Moore phoned us.'

'Oh?' I said, trying to look innocent.

'Tell him, John,' said Mum to Dad.

'She said that you played truant this afternoon,' Dad said.

'I didn't,' I said.

'Were you in school this afternoon?' asked Mum.

I was starting to feel uncomfortable, like one of those prisoners you see on TV who are being interrogated by the police. I wondered if I should ask for a lawyer.

'Yes,' I said.

Well, it was true. But then I realised that Miss Moore would have told them all about me being seen 'sneaking off with Edward Bates', as she called it. Though how anyone could call being dragged along a street by my collar 'sneaking off' puzzled me.

'But only at the end of the afternoon,' I added, keen to tell The Whole Truth and Nothing But The Truth.

'Where were you the rest of the afternoon?' demanded Mum.

'I was at the canal,' I admitted.

'Why?' asked Dad.

I hung my head and did my best to look ashamed. 'I don't know,' I said.

OK, as excuses go, it wasn't exactly the best. But if I'd told the truth, then there'd have been *real* trouble.

'Were you alone?' asked Dad.

As Miss Moore had told me I'd been seen with Banger Bates, and as Dad must have known that she'd told me, it seemed an odd question to ask. I wondered if he was trying to be a detective, or trying to catch me out with a trick question. That's one of the problems with adults who watch too many detective series on TV. They think they're detectives too.

'No,' I said.

'Who were you with?'

The sooner I could just get this over with and get told off and then get to my attic, the better.

'Banger Bates,' I said.

'Is that the boy known as Edward Bates?' demanded Mum.

'Yes.'

'Miss Moore says he is often in trouble,' said Mum.

'Yes, he is,' I agreed.

'Do you want to get in trouble?' asked Mum.

I wanted to say 'I'm already in trouble,' but I felt that would be pushing my luck. Instead, I shook my head. 'No,' I said, looking very sorry.

'Going off with bad boys and villains may seem very exciting,' said Dad. 'But they will all end up in prison. Do you want to go to prison?'

Prison? All I did was bunk off school for an hour and now Dad was talking about me going to prison!

'No,' I said.

'We have obviously been too lax with you, Dave,' said Mum in firm tones. 'We have given you too much freedom. It is our duty as parents to stop you going off the rails.'

'I'm sorry,' I said. 'I didn't mean to do anything wrong. It won't happen again.'

'No it won't,' agreed Mum. 'For the next week you aren't allowed out except to go to school.'

I looked at her, shocked. 'But I said I'd go to Paul's and help him with his project!'

'Miss Moore says that Paul lives just round the corner from this Edward Bates,' said Mum. 'Is that true?'

'Yes,' I said.

Mum shook her head. 'You are not going anywhere near that boy,' she said firmly. 'He will lead you into bad ways. Like today. And for the next week either your dad or I will take you to school and collect you afterwards.'

This shook me. 'Taken to school?' I echoed.

'And collected afterwards,' nodded Mum.

'No!' I burst out. 'That will make me look like one of the kids from Year 1! The other kids will make fun of me!'

'You should have thought of that before you sneaked off this afternoon,' said Mum. To Dad she added: 'Tell him, John.'

'We're collecting you from school to make sure temptation doesn't come your way,' Dad said.

I groaned. This was a nightmare. I nearly decided to tell them the truth, but then I thought about Banger bashing me up because of telling about him stealing the flesh-eating maggots from my locker, and decided against it.

'OK,' I sighed. I gave them both an appealing look. 'Is it all right if I take Fred for his walk?'

'No,' said Mum. 'Your dad will take him. You are to stay at home where we can keep an eye on you until we're sure you've decided to behave.'

Just then the phone rang. Dad picked it up.

'It's Paul for Dave,' he said, covering the receiver.

'Tell him you can't go out,' said Mum to me. 'You're staying in.'

'OK,' I said.

I took the phone. Mum and Dad stood looking at me.

'Hello?' I said.

'Are you on your own?' asked Paul.

'No,' I said. 'Mum and Dad are with me.'

'Can you get to your laptop?'

'Yes,' I said. 'It's in my room.'

'Go to the local news website,' he said.

'Why?' I asked.

He said something in a very low whisper.

'I can't hear you properly,' I told him.

'That's because I'm whispering,' he said. Then he lowered his voice again, and I had to strain to hear what he was saying. 'I don't want your mum and dad to hear.'

'To hear what?' I asked.

'The police are looking for you.'

CHAPTER 13

I stood there, my mind reeling. The police! Mum and Dad watched me, curious. I did my best to look untroubled, and forced a smile.

'No problem, Paul,' I said. 'I'll check that and get back to you.'

I hung up and turned to Mum and Dad.

'Paul wants me to check something for our Science project on my computer,' I explained.

Mum and Dad exchanged concerned looks.

'Aunt Dora's resting in your room,' said Dad. 'She went to lie down when she heard about you playing truant this afternoon. She was worried about the sort of person you were turning into. There has been lots of vandalism and car stealing near where she and Pete live.'

'I'm not turning into a car thief or a vandal!' I protested.

'Well, when you get your computer, don't say or do anything which might upset her,' warned Mum.

I left the kitchen, and bumped into Krystal. As I had suspected, Krystal had been hanging outside the kitchen, listening.

'My brother the gangster!' she mouthed at me, so that Mum and Dad wouldn't hear.

I pushed past her and headed upstairs. I had mixed feelings. Part of me wanted to rush up and switch on the computer and the local news website and find out what Paul meant about the police looking for me. The other part of me felt heavy-hearted at the unfairness of everything and just wanted to sit down on the stairs and cry.

I got to my room and knocked.

'Aunt Dora,' I called. 'It's Dave. I've come to get my laptop.'

'Wait a moment!' shrieked Aunt Dora from inside, her voice full of panic. There was a pause, then she

called out: 'You can come in now!'

I opened the door and went in. Aunt Dora was cowering as far away from the door as she could get without climbing out of the window. As I moved towards my computer, her eyes darted this way and that, as if she was looking for a weapon to defend herself. I can only guess that the way Dad and Mum had twisted the story they'd heard from Miss Moore had given her the impression I was now a cross between the Joker and a mad axeman.

I lifted my laptop off my table.

'Thank you, Aunt Dora,' I said politely.

I hurried up the stairs to the attic. Now I had my laptop I wanted to find out what Paul was talking about as quickly as possible. If the police really were looking for me then it wouldn't be hard for them to find me. All they had to do was ask Miss Moore, or Krystal, or anyone else who knew me.

There were lots of headlines on the local news website, but the only one related to me in any way said: 'POLICE HUNT BOY HOAXER.' Not that

I'd hoaxed anyone, but it was the only headline that had the words 'police' and 'boy' in it. All the others were about things like a cow who'd lived to be sixty-three, a woman who'd shoplifted a frozen chicken by putting it under her hat and been treated in hospital for hypothermia and a cat that played the violin.

The 'POLICE HUNT BOY HOAXER' item had a video link. I clicked it, and my blood froze.

The film showed the phone box where I'd made my 999 call. There was obviously a closed-circuit security camera aimed at the phone. Luckily the quality was pretty poor. It showed a grainy film of a boy walking backwards and forwards by the box, and then going to the phone and making a call, and then running away. It then went to a clip of a Police Inspector saying: 'This is the sort of hoax call that endangers lives. This kind of mindless hooliganism has to be stamped out. If anyone recognises the boy in this film, please contact …'

I switched it off, feeling sick. The boy in the film was me. Even though the quality was very grainy, Paul had recognised me. I wondered how many other people had?

In desperation, I thought about Mum and Dad sitting down to watch the local news on TV and seeing their son, with the Police Inspector appealing for anyone who knew the boy's identity to contact them. This would confirm their view that I'd gone over to the Dark Side and was just a few days away from being jailed for every crime under the sun.

There was only one answer.

I'd have to sabotage every TV set in the house.

CHAPTER 14

Luckily for me, the only television that mattered was in the living room. Krystal has got a TV in her room, but she never watches the news, only shows about clothes and fashion.

I took a screwdriver from my Science store and sneaked downstairs. I passed Krystal's room and heard her on her mobile to Shelly, telling Shelly about me, and how suddenly I'd become dangerous and a hoodie. I heard Aunt Dora crying in my room, so I knew she was safely out of the way. That just left Dad and Mum, and Dad was out taking Fred for his walk.

Mum was on the phone to my gran in the kitchen, also talking about me and how I'd suddenly become badly behaved. This was my chance. I hurried into the living room, looked around to make sure I couldn't be seen, then unplugged the TV from the socket on the wall. I took out the fuse from the plug, and then pushed the plug back into the socket.

FACTOID:
Accidents with Electricity
People should never take risks with electricity. In Britain every year about 8,000 people are killed or injured because of accidents in the home with electricity or electrical appliances.

I slipped the screwdriver and the fuse into my trouser pocket, and then wandered into the kitchen. Mum was just hanging up the phone. She looked at me questioningly.

'I've come to say sorry for causing all that trouble,' I said.

Mum smiled. 'See?' she said. 'I knew you were a good boy at heart, Dave. It's just a question of us being firm with you and keeping you on the straight and narrow.'

'So can I go to school on my own tomorrow?'

'No,' she said.

I headed back up the stairs to the attic with a heavy sigh. As I passed my door I could hear Aunt Dora shouting from inside my room. I decided she'd finally gone completely bats and was arguing with herself, but then I realised she was talking to Uncle Pete on her mobile.

'I don't care what you say, Pete!' she was squawking. 'You are a liar! You have broken my heart with your lies! I never want to see you again!'

Which meant she was going to be with us for even longer.

I was continuing on up the stairs to my attic, when the doorbell rang. Oh no! I thought. Someone had recognised me! It was the police come to arrest me!

I watched in terror as Mum went to the door and opened it. It was Paul.

'Can Dave come out, Mrs Dickens?' asked Paul.

'No,' said Mum firmly. She looked out into the

street and then asked him: 'Are you on your own?'

'Yes,' said Paul.

'In that case, you can come in,' she said. 'You are a good influence on him. Dave is upstairs.'

Paul and I went up to my attic.

'This room is great!' Paul beamed, looking around. 'At the top of the house, away from everybody! Brilliant! I wish I had a room like this!'

'You can have it,' I moaned. 'I want my own room back. What made you come round?'

'That thing on the local TV news,' said Paul. 'I wanted to know if you'd seen it, but I couldn't phone you and ask you because your mum would hear.'

I gestured at my laptop. 'Yes,' I said. 'I saw it.'

'It looks like you,' said Paul.

'No it doesn't,' I protested. 'It's too grainy, like all these CCTV films. It could be anyone.'

FACTOID:
CCTV Cameras
There are about 4.2 million CCTV cameras in Britain, which works out about one camera for every 14 people.

'I recognised you,' said Paul. 'And so did Suki. She was the one who saw it first and phoned me to tell me.'

'Why did she phone you?' I demanded. 'Why didn't she phone me?'

'In case your parents heard what she was saying.'

I sank down on my bed and put my head in my

hands with a heartfelt groan. I was trying to fool myself, but Paul was right. Anyone who knew me would have recognised me. My only hope was that hardly anyone would watch that particular edition of the local TV news.

'How are you going to stop your parents seeing it on the local news?' asked Paul.

'I …' I began.

'I thought we could blow your TV up,' Paul went on cheerfully. 'I saw this thing on *Top Gear* …'

'I've already fixed it!' I said, shutting him up.

Paul looked at me, surprised. 'How?'

'I took the fuse out of the plug on the TV,' I said.

Paul looked disappointed. 'That's not very exciting,' he said. 'Blowing it up would have been great!'

'I don't want to blow it up!' I said. 'I'd only get into even more trouble.'

'You could blame it on burglars,' suggested Paul.

'Why would burglars come into our house and blow up our TV?' I asked.

Paul shrugged. 'Why do people do anything?'

I glared at him. 'You only came round here to blow up our telly,' I said accusingly.

'No I didn't,' said Paul.

There was a pause.

'I was going to help *you* do it,' he admitted.

We headed for the door of my attic.

'What will you do tomorrow?' Paul asked. 'If someone has spotted you on the TV news? Will you go to school in disguise?'

'I can't,' I said. 'Mum's taking me.'

Paul gaped at me. 'Taking you to school?'

I nodded.

'Like an infant?' he said.

'All right, no need to rub it in,' I said grumpily. 'How did putting up the display go?'

'Good,' said Paul. 'My mobile of the universe looks really good.'

'What about my brain?' I asked.

Paul hesitated a second. 'Yes,' he said. 'That looks good as well.'

There was something in his voice which told me he was lying.

'What went wrong?' I asked suspiciously.

'Nothing,' he said quickly. Too quickly. Then he changed the subject and said: 'I'd better go home and see if you're on the late news.'

CHAPTER 15

I wanted to ask Paul more about the display and what had gone wrong with my model brain. But he was too quick, and hurried along the landing with me following. As we got to the bottom of the stairs, I saw Dad standing in the living room pointing the remote control at the TV and saying in a bewildered voice: 'I don't understand it. It was working this morning.'

He'd obviously come back from taking Fred for his walk. He hadn't been out with him for very long. When I take Fred for a walk we go to the park and Fred has a proper run, giving him the exercise a dog needs. Dad doesn't like taking Fred so he just goes to the end of the street where there's a patch of waste ground so Fred can do his business and then brings him back home again. I thought this was unfair on Fred, and I would have said so if I hadn't already been in a lot of trouble.

Mum was standing next to Dad, looking equally baffled.

'Maybe the satellite card's come out,' she said.

FACTOID:
Satellite TV
The first satellite TV signal was from the Telstar satellite in 1962. Satellites that send TV signals to Earth are in an orbit about 37,000km above the Earth's equator.

'I checked that,' said Dad. 'The TV's just dead. There's nothing at all. Not even that blue screen you sometimes get on the screen when it can't get a signal.'

'Maybe the plug's come out of the socket?' suggested Mum.

'I checked,' said Dad. 'The plug's firmly in.'

'I'm off now, Mrs Dickens, Mr Dickens,' said Paul.

I'd urged him to be very polite so that my parents would think I was being well-behaved too.

'Do you know anything about television sets, Paul?' asked Mum.

'Yes!' said Paul.

That's one of the problems with Paul. He thinks he knows all about technical things like space stations and computers, just because he's read about them. The trouble is, he doesn't know how to do things practically. He once took his mum's CD player apart to 'mend it' when it stopped working. When he put it back together again, he still had loads of parts left over that he couldn't fit in. Ever since, his mum has banned him from mending anything in their house.

'It's not working,' said Dad.

He handed Paul the remote control. I shot Paul a warning glance. I didn't want him saying anything that might reveal to them what I'd done. Paul saw my look, and nodded.

'Sorry, Mr Dickens,' he said, handing back the remote to Dad. 'I just realised what the time was. I promised Mum and Dad I wouldn't be long.'

'That's all right, Paul,' said Dad reluctantly.

'What a nice, well-behaved and respectful boy Paul is,' said Mum as Paul left. 'What a pity you can't be more like him, Dave, instead of hanging around with hoodies and truants.'

I had to bite my tongue to stop myself saying, 'Paul only came round here because he wanted to blow our telly up.' Instead, I said defensively: 'I *do* hang around with Paul.'

Dad was still holding the remote and shaking his head. 'I suppose we'll have to phone up the TV repair people,' he said.

'It would happen tonight,' complained Mum. 'There was a programme about famine in Africa I wanted to watch.'

I suddenly felt something hit my leg and land on the floor. I looked down. It was my screwdriver and the fuse from the TV plug. I hadn't pushed them into my pocket properly and they'd just fallen out.

Mum and Dad both stared at the screwdriver and the fuse. Dad looked bewildered, which is the way he often looks. But Mum was deeply shocked.

'Dave!' she said sharply. 'Are those what I think they are?'

'Er … they're from a Science experiment,' I said, snatching them up.

'Oh no you don't!' snapped Mum, and she grabbed me before I could make the stairs. 'John, check the plug on the TV. See if there's a fuse in it.'

She took the screwdriver from my hand and handed it to Dad.

Dad was slow to catch on. He looked at the screwdriver and said, 'Why? A fuse can't just jump out of a plug.'

'Exactly!' said Mum grimly, glaring at me.

As Dad unplugged the TV and unscrewed the plug I frantically tried to think of an excuse, but my mind was a blank. That's the problem with being an honest person. I'm no good at lying. Someone like Banger Bates lies all the time, and when he's found out he just protests and lots of times people actually believe him. If I lie, or if I'm feeling guilty, my ears go red. I guessed that right now my ears were red enough to light up an airport runway.

'There's no fuse in it!' announced Dad in surprise.

'Try this one,' said Mum, giving him the fuse.

Dad put the fuse in, screwed the plug back up and plugged it in. The TV immediately started working.

Mum's glare at me was now like an intense laser beam of fury. 'Do you have an explanation for this?' she demanded.

I'd never heard her voice this angry before. Not even when she sat down in a brand new dress on the collection of snot I'd accidentally left on a kitchen chair. It chilled me. I opened and closed my mouth, like a fish when it comes out of the water, but no words came out.

Dad was also now looking at me, realisation dawning. '*You* took the fuse out, Dave?' he exclaimed, stunned.

I gulped and nodded. 'It was a Science experiment,' I said lamely.

Mum's glare hardened into the sort you see on football managers when their favourite player gets sent off and a penalty is awarded against their team. For a moment I thought the top of her head was going to explode. She pointed upstairs.

'Get to your room!' she ordered angrily.

'I can't,' I defended. 'Aunt Dora's in it.'

'You know what I mean,' she grated. 'Get to the attic. And you don't leave there except to go to the toilet.'

'But ...' I began.

Mum's finger was still pointing up the stairs, her face a grim scowl. From now on anything I said would be a waste of breath. I gave a heavy sigh and began to trudge up the stairs. Mum and Dad stayed in the hall, watching me firmly all the way to make sure I didn't deviate and go and do something unlawful and hoodie-like to Krystal or Aunt Dora.

My life had just got even worse.

CHAPTER 16

That night I sat on the bed in the attic, thinking. There were definitely pigeons and other birds on the roof which kept walking about and scratching at the roof tiles and the guttering. At least, I hoped it was birds. It struck me that maybe it was rats. I'd read that rats could climb up the inside of a drainpipe. Maybe the noises I was hearing were rats.

Rats can get through very tiny spaces. I wondered if they could squeeze through the tiny gaps between the roof and the walls. If they could, then maybe they would find a way in to the attic.

And if it wasn't rats, it could be mice. They were even smaller and mice can definitely squeeze through the tiniest of cracks.

I sat and listened to the noises. I was in the worst

and unhappiest situation ever, and there seemed to be no way out. It was only a matter of time before someone recognised me on the grainy film and phoned the police. I wondered if the police would be offering a reward? If they did then I'd definitely be reported. I guessed that Krystal would be the first one to hand me in. If not Krystal, then one of her friends. Or one of the kids at my school.

The more I sat and thought about it, the surer I felt that by tomorrow someone would have given the police my name and address and they'd come round and arrest me. And what would Mum and Dad say to that?

Just the thought of this made me break out in a sweat. I felt sick. The feeling was so strong it made my worries over my Science Display seem like nothing. Something had gone wrong with my model of the human brain, I was sure of it. I could tell by the shifty way Paul said, 'Nothing,' when I asked him what the problem was.

It became clear to me that I couldn't stay here

any longer. I had to hide until the whole police business had blown over. Until the maggots were caught or died of natural causes. Until the police hunt for me became yesterday's news and I could walk around without fearing arrest. And until Aunt Dora left and I could have my old room back.

I looked at my watch. It was gone midnight. I went to the door of the attic room and opened it, and listened. There was no sound in the house. All the lights were off, except for the night light. Everyone was asleep in bed, except me.

I would run away.

OK, when I was found, or returned home, Mum and Dad would be angry all over again. But they would also be so relieved at me being alive that their main feeling would be Happiness. They'd hug me and maybe even give me presents to show how much they cared. Perhaps even some more bits for my microscope. Right now, if I stayed, all I'd get was Big Trouble.

It was a no-brainer. Running away was the only answer.

Mum and Dad's bedroom was directly below my attic room. Moving around as quietly as I could, I got dressed and packed a few things into a holdall: a change of pants and socks, and the only extra shirts I could find. That done, I crept downstairs, all the time listening out for any sounds.

As I tiptoed along the landing, I realised I needed to take my toothbrush with me. Hygiene is very important, and if you don't clean your teeth properly all sorts of germs and bacteria grow and live inside your mouth.

I crept into the bathroom. As I did, I heard a door open! Quickly I pushed the bathroom door shut and locked it.

There was a rattle as someone tried the door handle. Then Mum's voice said: 'Dave? Is that you in there?'

What could I do? If I didn't say anything she might think I was a burglar and call the police. But

FACTOID:
Brushing Teeth
If you don't brush your teeth properly, it leads to a build-up of germs and bacteria on your teeth, gums and tongue. Acid accumulates in your mouth and causes holes in your teeth. Bacteria on your gums can lead to gum disease, which can lead to your teeth falling out. The rotting food and bacteria in your mouth also causes very bad breath.

if I said it was me, she might wait to talk to me, and when I appeared she'd wonder what I was doing fully dressed and carrying a holdall.

'Dave?' she said again.

'Yes, Mum,' I said. 'It's me.'

'Well, don't make too much noise,' she said. 'You don't want to wake everyone up.'

And then I heard her feet move down the landing and her bedroom door close.

I nearly fell into the bath with relief.

I waited a few seconds. Then, as I headed for the

door, I stopped. Should I flush the toilet? If I did, would Mum come out and tell me off for making a noise? Or if I didn't, would she come out and tell me off for not flushing it?

I weighed it up and reached a decision. I flushed, and waited a few seconds to see if Mum came out.

She didn't.

I held my breath, gritted my teeth, unlocked the door and stepped out on to the landing. No one was about. All the doors were shut. But now I knew Mum was awake, I would have to move quickly.

I went downstairs as fast and as silently as I could. I'd decided that if she came out I was going to tell her I was going downstairs to get a drink of water, but she didn't appear. I reached the front door, slipped off the security chain, opened the door, stepped outside, and pulled the front door quietly but firmly shut behind me.

I had made it! I had escaped!

Fred came out of his kennel and began wagging his tail. I felt a tinge of sadness at the thought of leaving and not seeing him for a while, but I knew I couldn't take him with me. I knelt down and put my arms around him. Fred leaned into me and licked my face.

'I'm going away, Fred,' I whispered. 'I don't know for how long, or where, but I have to go. I'm in too much trouble to stay.'

Fred gave a little whine and nuzzled his face into my chest, as if he understood every word I

was saying and was showing he sympathised. As I knelt there and cuddled that good old friendly dog, it suddenly struck me that I didn't know where I was going. I couldn't just walk around the streets in case I was picked up by the police. I was already a wanted criminal. I looked at my watch. One o'clock in the morning. The trains would have stopped, and so would the buses.

I felt the first spot of rain. Then another. The rain felt like it was getting heavier. I had to find shelter, but where? I could hardly go to Paul's house, or Suki's, and ask if they'd take me in. I'd be soaked through, and their parents would be sure to phone up Mum and Dad and ask them what I was doing out at that hour. There was no one else I could think of to call on and ask for shelter. And I couldn't sleep in a doorway in this weather.

As the rain continued, I realised there was only one answer. I'd have to go back indoors and hope no one had heard me creep out. OK, it still meant the police might turn up and arrest me, but at least I wouldn't catch pneumonia and die.

I got up and patted Fred. 'Looks like I'm not leaving after all, Fred,' I said.

Fred wagged his tail and farted, a silent but noxious fart. I waved the smell away with my hand, gave a heavy sigh of doom, and trudged back towards the door. I dug into my pocket for my key … and then remembered I'd left it upstairs in the attic on the bedside table.

I was locked out.

For a moment I didn't know whether to be glad that I couldn't get back in, or angry. One thing was for sure: if I rang the bell and Mum or Dad had to get out of bed and come downstairs to let me in, I'd be in Really Big Trouble.

The rain was definitely getting heavier. I absolutely had to find somewhere to get out of the downpour.

Fred gave a little bark.

'Sshhh!' I said, and hurried over to shut him up.

Once again he wagged his tail and pressed his head against me.

As I patted him, I looked at his kennel. It was a big kennel, because Fred was a big dog. And there was a blanket in there. And it had a proper roof on it to make sure the rain couldn't get in. OK, it smelt of Fred's farts, which tended to linger long after he'd done them. But it would be dry in there. And I'd just have to make sure I got up early, before anyone came out and found me, and sneak back in. I didn't know *how* I was going to get into the house without being spotted, but right now – with the rain coming down and no key – that was a problem for the light of dawn.

CHAPTER 17

As dawn came the next morning, I crawled out of the kennel. My first problem was standing up. I'd fallen asleep in a corner and Fred had fallen asleep against me, pressing me into the kennel wall. The result was that my knees and back had got fixed into a bent position and when I tried to stand up straight I just fell over, like one of those puppets when its strings are cut.

I lay on the ground and Fred came out of his kennel and licked me on the face, the way that dogs do when they're trying to be helpful and comforting. Then he turned round because something more interesting was happening next to the kennel, a mouse or something, which put his bum in a straight line with my head. And, true to form, he farted.

That helped a lot more than him licking my face, because the power of the fart was enough to make me back away at speed, which got my legs moving; and pretty soon I was able to stand up again.

I heard footsteps, and turned to see the postman.

'Well,' he said cheerfully, 'you're up early!'

He handed me a bunch of envelopes, and a package. When I saw the words 'Transit Materials' stamped on the package, and realised that it looked exactly the same as the one containing the flesh-eating maggots that had been delivered before, I nearly fell over. Not *more* flesh-eating maggots?

FACTOID:
Post

Most things can be sent through the post. Sometimes there is a ban on anything that is said to be hazardous or inflammable. But even if a country's own postal service won't accept an object to send (e.g. a live animal), there will usually be a courier company that does.

I was standing there, the envelopes and package in my hand, wondering what to do, when I heard the front-door handle being rattled from the inside.

Oh no! I was going to be caught! Mum or Dad would see me and demand to know where I'd been all night. And whatever I said, they wouldn't believe me. They'd think I'd been out robbing banks with Banger Bates or something, and they'd put me under house arrest for the next twenty years! Even when I went to university, they'd take me there every day! My life was ruined for ever!

Quickly I ran round the corner of the house and peered around the wall. I was just in time. The door opened and Dad came out.

'Morning, Fred!' he said, and he headed towards his van.

I waited until he was busy looking for something in the back of the van, then I nipped round to the front door and inside the house. I dumped the envelopes on the doormat and headed for the stairs.

No one was around. Or if they were, they weren't making a noise.

I hurried up to the landing, and made it just as I heard Dad coming back into the house. Creeping past Mum and Dad's room, my room (now Aunt Dora's) and Krystal's room, I bolted up to my attic and put the package from Transit Materials on the table.

There was always the hope that it wouldn't be flesh-eating maggots. But when I looked at the package, it was exactly the same as the previous one. Same size, same type of envelope, same writing on the label, same name: DJ Dickens. But, just to check, I opened it.

Inside was a plastic container. And sure enough, inside the plastic I could see maggots wriggling.

Oh no! The whole nightmare was starting all over again!

The proper thing to do would be to hand them in to the police. But the police were already looking for me as a wanted criminal because of a hoax phone call about maggots. If I went into a police station and tried to hand the maggots over they'd arrest me on sight.

After what had happened before, I couldn't take the maggots with me to school.

I couldn't leave the package in the attic in case a small animal or bird got in and chewed through the plastic and let the maggots escape.

The only thing left was to hide it somewhere safe in the house where no one would find it, while I worked out what to do.

I sat and thought about it. If I left the package in the kitchen, or the bathroom, or the living room, someone would find it. For the same reason I couldn't chance hiding it in Mum and Dad's room, or Krystal's.

That left only one room: mine.

I didn't think Aunt Dora would go poking around in my room in case she found something shocking. She knew about my collection of Science specimens, and I bet she hadn't opened any cupboards or drawers since she'd arrived. So hiding the maggots in my room was the safest bet.

I stood listening. I could hear voices coming from downstairs in the kitchen: Mum and Aunt Dora. Which meant that my room was free!

It was a matter of seconds to rush down to my room, nip in, open my wardrobe, hide the package right at the back and then hurry out again before Aunt Dora returned and caught me.

I was in luck. Aunt Dora was still downstairs arguing with Mum. I heard my name mentioned and realised they were arguing about me. I crept to the top of the stairs so I could hear better.

'Dave is not on drugs!' I heard Mum say, very crossly.

'You don't know that,' responded Aunt Dora. 'The way he's been acting is very unlike him.'

'Dave is only eleven,' pointed out Mum.

'There are cases of children as young as nine being on drugs,' retorted Aunt Dora. 'They get in with bad company. And you said yourself that Dave has got in with this dreadful Edward Bates boy.'

'That doesn't mean he's doing drugs!' defended Mum.

'The only way to find out the truth is to get him checked by a doctor,' said Aunt Dora. 'They'll take blood tests and …'

'I'm not taking my son to a doctor to check for drug use!' snapped Mum. 'I know what's causing this: he's being led astray. Unfortunately, Dave is weak and easily led. He gets that from your side of the family.'

'How dare you!' said Aunt Dora, shocked.

To be honest, hearing this cheered me up. Especially hearing Mum defend me against the charge of using drugs. I know what terrible things drugs can do to the human body from my Science researches. Only complete idiots do drugs.

'Anyway, you don't need to take him to a doctor,' continued Aunt Dora. 'Just take a piece of his hair and send it to a lab. They can test it for drug use. If people are using drugs it shows up in their hair.'

'I am not sending a piece of Dave's hair to any lab!' snapped back Mum. 'Now, if you'll excuse me, Dora, I have to get on because I'm taking Dave to school this morning.'

'What are you doing sneaking around?' barked Krystal's voice behind me.

I jumped so high, I nearly fell down the stairs. Recovering, I turned round. She was standing with her dressing gown on and her towel draped over her arm.

'Nothing,' I said.

She glared at me. 'If you take anything from my room I shall tear your head off and feed it to that rotten dog,' she threatened.

'Why would I want to take anything from your room?' I demanded, bewildered.

'Because that's what your sort does,' she said. 'Criminals. Bad boys. We've got them at our school and they're stupid. They take everything, useful or not.'

'I don't want anything that's in your room,' I assured her firmly.

And I meant it. Krystal's room is filled with fluffy pink things and pictures of boy bands.

'You'd better not,' she said. Then she stopped and looked at me suspiciously. 'Have you just been in that bathroom?' she demanded.

'No,' I said.

'Good,' she said. 'You make it stink.'

CHAPTER 18

Going to school was so embarrassing. Mum drove me there. All the way to school I kept wondering what I could do to pretend to people that she wasn't actually taking me to school like an infant, but just giving me a lift on her way somewhere else. I thought through the things I could shout out as she drove off, like, 'Thanks for the lift, Mum! Lucky you were on your way to the supermarket!' But what would I shout out when she dropped me off at school the next day? And the day after?

The journey was made worse because Aunt Dora said she wanted a lift into town, which meant we were fifteen minutes late leaving because of her checking everything twice, like had she got her purse with her (she had), did she have her shopping list (she did), and so on. As a result, we got caught up in traffic and I was going to be late. At one point, when we were sitting in a traffic jam and going nowhere, I suggested to Mum that it would be quicker for me to get out and walk, but Mum insisted that she wanted to see me actually go in. I pointed at the clock, which showed five minutes to nine.

'I'm going to be in trouble for being late,' I told Mum. 'And it's not my fault.'

Mum just scowled and ground her teeth, looked at Aunt Dora – who was sitting in the back seat – in the rear-view mirror and ignored me. Then she said:

'Now you're not to get into any trouble today. I've told Miss Moore to phone me and let me know if you do anything wrong.'

'I won't,' I assured her. 'Except be late for school.'

Once again, Mum ignored my complaint. 'And you're not to have anything to do with that boy Bates,' she added.

'I can't help it,' I said. 'He sits on the same table as me in class.'

'Miss Moore says she's going to move you to another table,' Mum said.

That cheered me up a bit. Being on the same table as Banger was a nightmare. He was always trying to kick me and the other kids under the table. Luckily, because he wasn't very coordinated, he usually ended up kicking himself, but sometimes he got me.

We got out of one traffic jam and almost straight away ended up in another.

Mum would never know that I'd nearly run away. Instead of taking me to school today, she and Dad could have been holding a TV press conference, begging me to return home. But then I wondered if they would have. Neither of them had noticed my absence. If I'd started walking last night instead of crawling into Fred's kennel, I could have been miles and miles away by now, and they wouldn't have known, because nobody had bothered to come into the attic room to talk to me. They hadn't come in to say goodnight. They hadn't even come in to tell me off. They'd just ignored me.

I was The Invisible Boy.

Finally we reached the school. We were five minutes late. Mum pulled up in a sort of parking area nearly opposite the school.

'You don't have to sit here and watch me go in,' I appealed to her.

'I'm not going to,' she said.

I brightened up. Only a few kids would see that my mum had brought me to school. But her next words sent a chill right through me.

'I'm coming in to school with you.'

'What?!' I stared at her in shock. 'Why?'

'Because I need to explain to Miss Moore why you're late this morning,' she said. Again, she shot a look of annoyance into the rear-view mirror at Aunt Dora. 'And I said I was going to take you to school, and that's exactly what I'm going to do.'

She got out. I noticed that Aunt Dora was also

getting out of the back of the car.

'There's no need for you to come, Dora,' said Mum.

'Yes there is,' said Dora. 'If I'm left in the car alone it could get hijacked. Or a lorry might hit it. Or vandals might come along and attack it. Or …'

'I don't have time for this,' sighed Mum wearily. 'All right, you can come in as well.'

As the three of us walked in through the school gates, my heart sank. On one level it was good that everyone had already gone in, because no one saw me being brought to school by my mum and my aunt. But on the other hand, we would be walking in just as some of the classes would be passing through the Reception Area on their way to Assembly, which meant that *someone* would see me, and word would soon spread: *Dave Dickens was brought to school by his mum and his aunt.*

As I followed Mum into the school building, I felt a sharp pain in the top of my head. I turned round. Aunt Dora was hiding something in her handkerchief. She'd pulled a piece of hair out so she could get it tested it for drugs!

I wanted to say something sharp to Mum about this, but she was already on her way along the corridor to my classroom. I followed her. But then I saw our class's Science Display and my model brain. I stopped dead in horror. The jelly had melted! My model brain was just a blobby shapeless lump of pink on a plate, sitting in a squidgy wet pink liquid!

'Aaargh!' I croaked, and pointed at my melted model in shock.

Aunt Dora leapt back. 'Wha … wha …?' she babbled, looking at me in alarm.

'My brain has melted!' I burst out.

'Help!' shrieked Aunt Dora. 'It's the drugs! They've melted his brain!'

And she began to back away from me, towards our Science Display table. For a second I was baffled. Then I realised what she meant. She thought I'd taken so many drugs my *real* brain had melted.

'No!' I said, trying to explain. 'My brain on the table!'

And I moved forward, pointing at the Science Display table behind her.

'Don't come near me!' shrieked Aunt Dora in panic. 'Help! He's high on drugs!'

I put on my most sincere face and moved towards the table to show her that I was talking about my melted *model* brain.

'Aaargh!' yelled Aunt Dora.

She jumped back and landed right on the Science Display, tipping the table up. My model brain – now mostly squidgy pink jelly and liquid – rolled off its plate and landed on the floor by her feet, with quite a bit of it going in her shoes.

'Yurk!' Aunt Dora squealed, trying to get out of the way. But her feet slipped on the sloppy jelly and she began to fall. Frantically she grabbed at something to stop herself falling, and her clutching hands caught hold of Paul's moving mobile of the Universe.

Down she went on to the floor, taking Paul's model with her, and most of the rest of the stuff on the display table. There was a bang as she landed on the big balloon that Paul had hung up depicting the sun, and the balloon disappeared into a tiny shrivelled piece of rubber.

By now, all this shouting had brought everyone out of their classes to see what was going on. What they saw was Aunt Dora sitting in a puddle of wet pink jelly with a load of different-coloured balls on strings hanging around her neck and shoulders, and other pieces of our Science Display scattered around her.

'My model of the universe!' came an anguished cry.

Paul was looking in horror at his wrecked model. The rest of my class, and Miss Moore, and Mum, were standing with him, goggling at the scene.

Mum was the first to recover.

'Dave!' she barked angrily.

'It wasn't me!' I protested. 'I didn't do anything!'

At that moment one of the glass display jars

containing Suki's insects fell off the table and landed by Aunt Dora, and broke, and a cockroach came out and began to climb over her knee. Aunt Dora's scream made everyone in the whole school take cover with their hands over their ears.

FACTOID:
Cockroaches
A cockroach can live for up to a month after losing its head. Then it will die of thirst.

I looked at Mum. 'If you hadn't insisted on bringing me to school, none of this would have happened,' I pointed out.

Mum glowered at me as if this was still all my fault.

'We'll talk about this later, Dave,' she said. 'When I come to collect you after school.'

Then she grabbed Dora by the elbow and hauled her to her feet.

'Come on, Dora,' she said. 'I think it's time we left.'

CHAPTER 19

One good thing that came out of all this was that Miss Moore let me, Paul and Suki off lessons before break to put the Science Display back together again. She obviously let Paul and Suki do it because their exhibits had been damaged, and I guess she let me do it with Paul and Suki because she felt a little bit sorry for me. It must have been pretty obvious to her that Aunt Dora had destroyed our display. And it was Miss Moore's fault that Mum and Aunt Dora had turned up today.

Paul was pretty upset about his wrecked model of the universe, but we worked together and were able to reconstruct it so it looked the same as before, but with a different-coloured balloon for the sun. We went round to all the other classes looking for a big red balloon, but the only big one we could get was from Mrs Walton's, and it was yellow. When Suki pointed out that the sun would really be yellow rather than red because of its hot gases, Paul cheered up.

FACTOID:
The Sun

75% of the sun is hydrogen. Most of the rest of it is helium. Oxygen, carbon and iron make up less than 2% of the sun's mass.

We found Suki's cockroach and another jar to put it in, so that was all right.

The only real casualty was my model brain, which had been completely destroyed. Paul and Suki suggested I bring in the model brain that I'd got from the toyshop instead. I pointed out that it wasn't one I'd made, and it didn't wobble like a real brain, but they said that as no one was allowed to touch the display, it wouldn't really matter. And

I could always make another brain for another display later, and one that wouldn't melt. So that was what we agreed.

I learnt from Paul and Suki that Banger Bates wasn't in school today. The last time I'd seen him, he'd been standing up to his neck in water in the canal, and I wondered whether he'd caught a cold. But as we fixed up Paul's universe model, Paul told me the real reason.

'Banger's got a big boil on his forehead. I heard Mrs Payne telling Miss Moore.'

'What sort of boil?' I asked.

'How do I know?' said Paul. 'Just a boil.'

'You don't think it might be the maggots?' asked Suki, worried.

'That's what I was just thinking,' I agreed. 'Maybe they didn't all fall off in the canal. Maybe one of them got stuck in his hair or something and has worked its way into his head, and this thing that looks like a boil is actually the maggot starting to eat its way out.'

A boil is caused when the root of a hair follicle in the skin becomes infected. This leads to pus and dead tissue, and is very painful. A network of boils together is called a carbuncle.

'Ugh! Yurk! Gross!' said Paul.

'It's possible,' said Suki, looking worried. 'You have to tell someone, Dave.'

'I tried to, and look what happened!' I pointed out. 'The police are looking for me! If I try and tell anyone else, I'm going to be arrested for certain! And, what's worse, more maggots arrived today!'

'What?' said Suki, shocked.

Briefly I told them about the latest parcel.

'But why would they send more?' asked Suki, baffled.

'It's part of a plan by aliens to take over the world,' said Paul.

'It is not aliens!' I said. 'They were sent by this TV company!'

'Which could well be run by aliens,' said Paul. 'This could all be part of their big plan. They get people to send them their names and addresses, and then send them loads of packets of flesh-eating maggots.'

Miss Moore arrived.

'You need to hurry up and get the display finished,' she said. 'After break we have Literacy, and you'll need to be in class for that.'

'If we haven't finished by the end of break, can we do it during lunch?' asked Paul.

'We want it to look good,' added Suki. 'After all, our class's reputation is at stake with this display.'

Which I thought was a very clever thing to say. Miss Moore hesitated, then nodded.

'All right,' she said. 'But you only have until the end of lunch.'

She went back to our class. Me and Paul grinned at Suki.

'Clever thinking, Suki!' said Paul. 'Finding a way to stay in at lunch.' And he chuckled as he mimicked Suki saying: '"After all, our class's reputation is at stake with this display."' He laughed again. 'Brilliant!'

Suki looked at us, puzzled. 'But I meant it!' she said. 'Our reputation should be important to us!'

Paul and I exchanged shamefaced looks at this.

'Of course it is!' I agreed. 'That's what Paul and me meant.'

And we got on with fixing the display.

CHAPTER 20

Once Paul and Suki had told me about Banger and the boil, all I could think about for the rest of the morning was the maggot eating its way through Banger's head, and what to do about the parcel of yet more flesh-eating maggots sitting in my wardrobe in Aunt Dora's room. I kept thinking about it during our Literacy lesson, which was unfortunate because when Miss Moore snapped at me: 'What's the answer, Dave?' I replied, 'Maggots,' and everyone laughed, because the question she'd asked was: 'What is the proper term for speech marks?'

Actually, I didn't know the answer to the question anyway.

After we'd eaten our sandwiches at lunch, Paul, Suki and me were back at the display table in the

Reception Area, putting the finishing touches to our repaired display. And I was able to talk about Banger again.

'There are two things we have to do,' I told them. 'One, we have to find out if the boil on Banger's head is really a boil, or if it's a maggot eating its way out of his head. Two, we have to hand in the new packet of maggots to the police. The trouble is, Mum's coming to pick me up from school so I can't go round to Banger's house. And even if she wasn't coming, if she heard I'd been to see Banger I'd be in Big Trouble, because they think he's turning me into a hoodie. And I can't show my face anywhere near a police station because I'd be arrested for what they said was a hoax phone call.'

For a moment I felt like crying. I almost told them about spending the night in Fred's kennel and waking up so stiff I couldn't stand up, and how no one had noticed I wasn't at home. But the very thought of it just made me want to cry even more. So instead I just let out a heavy, heartfelt sigh. My lower lip was trembling, and I had to bite the inside of my cheeks to stop my huge feelings of unhappiness from turning into proper tears.

FACTOID:
Crying
Emotional tears contain different chemicals from tears caused by things such as peeling onions. Emotional tears have hormones in them. Getting rid of these hormones by crying makes people feel better.

'I'll do it,' said Paul.

'So will I,' said Suki.

I was stunned. This was the last thing I had expected either of them to say.

'What?' I said.

'I'll take the maggots to the police,' said Paul. 'I'll come round to your house later and collect them. I'll tell the police I found the package lying in the street.'

'You'd better make sure you take your name and

address off the package,' Suki said to me. Turning to
Paul, she added: 'And you'd better tell them you saw
a programme about flesh-eating maggots on the
TV and you think that's what they are, otherwise
they might just throw them away.'

'I was going to do that anyway,' said Paul,
sounding a bit put out. Then he asked Suki: 'If I'm
doing that, what are you going to do?'

'I'll go round to Banger's house and take a look
at his boil,' said Suki.

Paul and I looked at Suki with a new sense of awe and admiration. We both knew she was clever, and she was long-suffering, as we had seen by the way she looked after her dreadful little brother. But this was being really really brave. Even the police and the local council were afraid to go to Banger's house. And to go there knowing that she'd actually find Banger there, and possibly his dad as well …

'You are the bravest person I have ever met, Suki,' I said.

Paul looked at me, annoyed. 'What about me?' he demanded.

'You are the cleverest person about the planets and science fiction,' I told him.

Paul hesitated, then nodded. 'Yes I am,' he said. 'Thank you.' Then he turned to Suki and said: 'Dave's right. What you're going to do is really brave.'

'I'm just doing the right thing,' Suki said. 'We have to know if the maggots have infected Banger. And if they have, we have to save him.'

CHAPTER 21

At the end of school I walked out of the gates and saw Mum waiting for me with all the other mums and dads. It was so humiliating. All the other kids whose parents were waiting for them were Year 1s and 2s, the really little kids who were still learning to walk properly – and I was in Year 6. I thought of trying to pretend that it wasn't Mum who'd come to collect me, but me who'd insisted Mum came to the school so I could protect *her* from muggers and criminals, but I knew no one would believe me. So I just put my head down and followed her to the car.

Mum didn't speak at all on the drive home, so I knew I was still in her bad books. When we got home, she said: 'I'm sorry we have to do this, Dave, but it's for your own good. We're trying to protect you from yourself.'

I felt too humiliated and unhappy to reply. I just wondered how long this was going to last. I felt like a prisoner.

As I walked slowly past Krystal's room, her door opened and she leapt out, hands ready to grab me by the hair. I dodged out of her way and snatched a tissue from my pocket and held it out towards her.

'This tissue contains fresh snot,' I warned. 'If you grab me, the snot will get stuck on your hand.'

FACTOID:
Snot
Humans swallow about a litre of snot a day.

Krystal recoiled, but the expression of fury stayed on her face.

'You have ruined my reputation with all my friends!' she snarled.

'Just because Shelly doesn't like me …' I began.

'Not just Shelly!' she snapped. 'Everyone recognised you on the TV news last night and now everyone knows that my brother is a vandal and a delinquent and a criminal and is going to jail!'

I was in shock. Her friends had seen it!

'It wasn't me!' I blurted out.

'Yes it was,' said Krystal. 'You wait till Mum finds out!'

'What are you two doing up there?' called Mum from downstairs. 'I hope you're not fighting again!'

For one awful moment I thought that Krystal was going to say something to Mum about my being caught on the CCTV camera, but then the doorbell rang, and Mum headed off to open the door.

'I wish the police would come and arrest you and then you'd be out of the house!' hissed Krystal.

'Then why don't you tell Mum?' I challenged her.

Krystal scowled some more, and then spat: 'Because you are my brother! And families have to look after each other. That's what Shelly says.'

With that she stomped back inside her room and slammed her door. Stunned, I stared at her closed door. Krystal was doing something nice for me! All right, it wasn't so much doing something as *not* doing something. And even though it was her friend Shelly who'd told her about 'families looking after each other', as a rule Krystal never took any notice of her when it came to treating me nicely.

Suddenly I decided that I really liked Shelly. OK, she was an airhead who thought that everything in the world was 'lovely'. But if something she said had saved me from being shopped by Krystal, she could stay an airhead as far as I was concerned.

It was then I became aware of the voices from downstairs, and realised that one of them belonged to Uncle Pete, Aunt Dora's husband. It was obviously him who'd just arrived.

'Dave!' called Mum. 'Can you come down here?'

I went down, passing Uncle Pete on his way up. He looked really really miserable. But then, if I was married to Aunt Dora, I think I'd look miserable too.

'Hello, Dave,' he said sadly.

'Hello, Uncle Pete,' I said.

Pete trudged past me and stopped outside my room. He knocked at the door.

'Dora,' he called. 'It's me! Pete!'

'Go away!' called Aunt Dora from inside my room.

I stood on the stairs, curious to see what was going to happen next.

'Dave! I want to see you NOW!'

Mum's sharp voice jerked me back to my own problems. I had to do everything Mum said before one of her friends told her they'd recognised me on the TV news. It was only a matter of time before that happened.

At the bottom of the stairs, I was immediately grabbed by Mum and hauled into the kitchen.

'Uncle Pete's here to talk to Dora,' she hissed.

'Yes, I worked that out,' I said.

'So I want you to stay out of their way. With a bit of luck Pete will be able to persuade Dora to go back home with him.'

I looked at her, puzzled. 'Aunt Dora said he'd fallen in love with a dentist and had abandoned her,' I said. 'Why is he coming round and asking her to go back?'

'I don't know,' said Mum. 'It may have been this business with the dentist was just an infatuation. But we must do everything we can to help get Dora out of the house.'

I shook my head doubtfully. 'She wasn't even opening the door to him,' I told her.

'She will,' said Mum, but with a confidence I don't think she really had.

The door bell rang again, and my heart gave a jump. Was this going to be one of Mum's friends calling to report that they'd seen me on the TV news?

Mum opened the door. It was Paul.

'Hello, Mrs Dickens,' he said. 'Is Dave in?'

'Come in, Paul,' she said.

Paul walked in and mouthed: 'The maggots?' at me.

I turned to Mum. 'Mum, Paul and I need to go upstairs. I've got some stuff in the attic that we're working on for our school project.'

Mum hesitated. She had a big dilemma. On one hand, Pete was on the landing trying to talk to Dora through the door and we'd have to go past him. On the other hand, she was trying to encourage me to be a Good Boy, which meant making sure I did well at school. Finally she nodded.

'All right,' she said. 'But don't upset things as you go upstairs.'

'What things?' asked Paul.

'Nothing important,' said Mum crisply.

On the landing, me and Paul found Uncle Pete kneeling by the door with his mouth pressed to the keyhole.

'I love you, Dora,' he was saying.

'This is Paul, Uncle Pete,' I said.

'Hello,' said Paul.

'Hello,' said Uncle Pete. He returned to cooing through the keyhole. 'My life is empty without you, Dora.'

We stepped carefully over Uncle Pete's legs and continued towards the attic stairs.

'What's all that about?' asked Paul.

'I'll tell you when we get upstairs,' I said.

CHAPTER 22

Once we were inside my attic room, I filled Paul in on Uncle Pete coming round to appeal to Dora to return home.

'Why?' asked Paul.

I shook my head and sighed. 'I have no idea,' I said.

'Anyway, if you give me the maggots I'll take them to the police,' said Paul.

'I can't just yet,' I told him. 'I hid them in my wardrobe in my room, and Dora's in there, with Uncle Pete outside.'

'Oh,' said Paul. He frowned. 'How long will we have to wait before you can get in there?'

'I don't know,' I admitted. 'If he gets her to go home with him, it could take ages because she has to double-check everything first. But if she tells him to get lost, it could be quick. He'll go, and then – with a bit of luck – she'll go downstairs to moan to Mum about him.'

Just then Paul's mobile rang. 'Hello?' he said. He listened for a bit, nodding all the while, then he said: 'OK, I'll tell him.'

He hung up. '"That was Suki,' he said. 'She couldn't get in to see Banger.'

'Why not?' I asked.

'Because there was a TV crew at his house: cameras, sound, vans, the lot.'

I looked at Paul in horror.

'Maybe the maggots did it!' I gasped. 'They ate him after all! The TV news people must have heard about it and went round to his house! I'll bet there's just a heap of bones lying there!'

'Dave!' Krystal suddenly shouted. 'Your school's on the TV!'

'Krystal!' Mum yelled angrily. 'Uncle Pete and Aunt Dora are trying to talk!'

'But it's Dave's school!' Krystal called back. 'Something really dreadful's happened!'

'It must be the maggots!' I groaned.

'We'd better go and see what's happening,' said Paul. 'Won't it be incredible if those maggots have eaten Banger!'

'It will be terrible!' I said. 'I could get charged with murder!'

'Why?' asked Paul, baffled. 'He took them from you.'

I gestured anxiously at my laptop. 'We could watch the news up here on this,' I suggested.

Paul shook his head. 'By the time that gets started up, the news item will be over. Come on! Let's go downstairs and find out what's happening!'

With that he rushed out of the attic. I hesitated. This wasn't going to be good news. But whatever it was, it all had to come out sooner or later.

I hurried after Paul, down the stairs and along the landing. Uncle Pete was still kneeling by the door of my bedroom talking through the keyhole.

'That dentist meant nothing to me!' he appealed. 'I was just flattered because she told me I had the teeth of a much younger man! Ow!'

FACTOID:
Teeth Hygiene
More microbes live in your mouth than there are humans on Earth. The microbes include hundreds of bacteria. The bacteria that rots teeth is called Streptococcus Mutans.

'Sorry, Uncle Pete,' I apologised, lifting up my foot where I'd accidentally trodden on his ankle.

'Don't you go "Ow!" at me!' shouted Aunt Dora through the closed door.

'I wasn't saying "Ow" to you, my darling,' said Pete. 'I was saying "Ow" because Dave trod on my ankle.'

'You're just saying that in the hope I'll feel sympathy for you!' snapped Aunt Dora. 'Well I don't!'

I joined Mum, Krystal and Paul in the living room, where they were all watching the TV. Banger's dad was standing in front of his house looking at the camera. Next to him stood Banger with a big boil on his head, looking very miserable.

Banger's dad pointed at the boil on Banger's head.

'My son was attacked by flesh-eating maggots!' he announced. 'This is what they did to him! These dangerous flesh-eating maggots were forced on him by another boy who brought them to school.'

'So what do you plan to do, Mr Bates?' the interviewer asked.

'We are going to sue the school, and the boy,' said Banger's dad. 'I believe the compensation for what we as a family have suffered should be in the region of a million pounds.'

A million pounds?!

The room started to swim. I clutched at the nearest chair to support myself.

'Flesh-eating maggots!' Mum said in horror. 'I wonder who this boy was who brought them to your school, Dave?'

'It was me,' said a faint voice. With a shock, I realised the voice was mine.

Mum stared at me, her mouth open. Finally she managed to speak.

'You?!'

'It wasn't Dave's fault, Mrs Dickens,' said Paul. 'This television company sent them to him and he didn't know what to do with them, so he took them in to school, and Banger stole them from him.'

'What?' asked Mum, looking more bewildered than ever. She sat down heavily in a chair.

Krystal's eyes narrowed and she glared at me dangerously. 'You had flesh-eating maggots in this house?' she snarled. 'Killer maggots that could have eaten me?'

'No,' I whispered. 'I took them to school.'

As best I could, I told them about the TV programme on the flesh-eating maggots, and my emailing them asking for a copy of the programme, and how instead they'd sent me a packet containing actual flesh-eating maggots. I told them about Banger stealing them from my locker and giving them to his dad for fishing. And how he'd dragged me along to the canal to stop his dad using them.

'So you weren't playing truant?' asked Mum.

I felt like a huge weight had lifted off me. 'No,' I said.

'But why didn't you tell us, instead of letting us think you were becoming a delinquent?'

I couldn't speak.

'Because he was worried that Banger would beat him up if he said what really happened,' Paul put in. 'Banger is a bully and everyone's afraid of him.'

Mum took all this in. 'Is this true?' she asked me.

'Yes,' I said miserably.

Mum hesitated. Then she stepped forward. For a moment I thought she was going to bash me round the head. Instead, she hugged me.

'My poor baby boy,' she said. And she squeezed me tighter.

I looked at Paul, who seemed to find this very funny, and at Krystal, who mimed poking her fingers down her throat to show it made her feel sick. I hastily disentangled myself from Mum's hug.

'I'm all right, Mum,' I said quickly. 'I know I should have said all this before, but …'

Mum went to hug me again, but this time I dodged her arms.

'Anyway, it's all over now,' Mum said.

'No it isn't,' said Krystal. She pointed at the TV. 'He said he's going to sue Dave for a million pounds.'

Mum's put on her Very Determined expression. 'I'd like to see him try,' she said grimly. 'Don't worry, Dave. Me and your dad will deal with this.'

'Great!' said Paul cheerfully. 'So there's only the other maggots to deal with.'

Mum and Krystal looked at Paul, puzzled.

'What other maggots?' Mum asked.

'The ones hidden in Dave's wardrobe,' said Paul.

At that moment there came the most terrifying, ear-splitting scream from upstairs. And then we heard Aunt Dora yell in a panic:

'There are MAGGOTS IN HERE!'

CHAPTER 23

We ran up the stairs. Well, when I say 'we', me and Mum ran up the stairs. Krystal and Paul stayed firmly in the living room.

The door of my bedroom was open. Dora was outside on the landing, banging at her clothes and shrieking: 'Maggots! Maggots!' while Uncle Pete stood there looking completely bewildered.

And there *were* maggots, crawling over the carpet.

'Stay away from them!' shouted Mum.

'I found a packet in the wardrobe!' screamed Aunt Dora. 'I opened it because I thought it might be drugs!'

'You stupid woman!' yelled Mum. 'They're flesh-eating maggots!'

'What?!' gaped Uncle Pete. 'Flesh-eating …?!'

As Aunt Dora realised what the maggots actually were, she gave a scream that nearly blew my eardrums out and ran down the stairs at enormous speed, as if Running Down the Stairs had become an Olympic event and she was going for gold.

Mum had already taken her mobile out and was dialling 999.

'Emergency!' she said. 'We have an invasion of flesh-eating maggots inside our house, and there are people at risk.' And she gave our address.

'I think we all ought to go downstairs and wait for the emergency services to arrive,' Mum told me and Uncle Pete as she snapped her phone shut. 'And no one is to open any doors to the outside. We can't risk the maggots getting out into the outside world.'

When we got downstairs, an amazing sight met our eyes. Aunt Dora was taking her clothes off. She had already taken off her blouse and skirt and thrown them on the floor. Paul and Krystal were goggling at her.

'Dora!' shouted Mum. 'What do you think you're doing?'

'The maggots!' moaned Aunt Dora. 'They're in my clothes!'

'No they're not!' snapped Mum. 'Put your clothes on at once!'

'I'm not putting them on again!' wailed Aunt Dora. 'There could be maggots in them!'

The doorbell went. Mum turned to Pete.

'Make sure she doesn't take anything else off!' she ordered.

By now Aunt Dora was down to her bra and pants, and looked as if she was about to unhook her bra. Uncle Pete rushed over to her and threw his coat over her.

'That's enough, Dora!' he said.

Mum looked at me and Paul. 'You two come with me,' she ordered.

'I'll come with you as well,' said Krystal, looking at Aunt Dora and Pete with some distaste.

We all went to the door. Two uniformed police

officers, a man and a woman, were standing outside.

'Is this the Dickens household?' asked the man.

'Yes,' said Mum. 'And I have to admit you were a lot quicker than I thought you'd be.' She looked past them at their patrol car and frowned. 'Is your special equipment in the car?'

The two police officers exchanged puzzled looks.

'What special equipment would that be, ma'am?' asked the woman officer.

'To get the maggots,' said Mum.

'Maggots?' echoed the man. 'We're not here for maggots.'

'Then what are you here for?' demanded Mum.

The man officer straightened up and put on an official face. 'We are here because we have received information that this is the address of one David Dickens, whom we believe made a malicious hoax phone call ...'

'Dave?' Mum said, looking at me in shock.

'It wasn't a hoax,' I said. 'I was trying to tell them

about the flesh-eating maggots!'

At this the two police officers looked even more bewildered.

'*Flesh-eating* maggots?' repeated the woman officer. 'What flesh-eating maggots?'

Suddenly we heard the sound of sirens approaching at speed. The next second, a load of vehicles had skidded to a halt at the end of our front garden. There were two police cars, three ambulances, a fire engine, and a big black van with the words 'Environmental Protection' on the side. The doors of this black van sprang open and four figures jumped out, dressed in hazard suits which covered

FACTOID:
Flu
Flu pandemics can spread worldwide and kill millions of people. The flu pandemic of 1918 killed more than 50 million people, many times the number that died during the whole of the First World War, which lasted from 1914 to 1918.

them completely from head to foot.

A voice from a loudspeaker boomed out from one of the police cars: 'Go back inside the house!'

Mum, me, Paul and Krystal obediently stepped back inside. The two uniformed police officers stood uncertainly in the doorway. Then they headed back to their own patrol car.

'Stop!' shouted the voice from the loudspeaker.

The two police officers stopped.

'Go inside the house!' ordered the voice.

'But this is nothing to do with us!' appealed the man officer.

'We cannot risk contamination!' called the voice. 'Step inside the house and await instructions.'

The two officers trudged unhappily into our house and joined us. My last sight of the outside world was of Fred hastily disappearing into his kennel at all the commotion as the four people wearing hazard suits came running in and shut the door firmly behind them.

'No one is to leave this house until we have given

the all-clear!' said one. His voice sounded really weird, coming through a sort of microphone on his helmet.

'This is just like the ending of *Curse of the Maggot People*!' whispered Paul excitedly. 'This is what happened there!'

'You will please all go into the same room!' commanded the voice. 'That one!'

A silver metallic gloved finger pointed towards

the living room. We all went in. Uncle Pete was still trying to put his coat over Aunt Dora, and Aunt Dora was still throwing it off and leaping about the room in her bra and pants.

The two uniformed officers exchanged looks.

'What's she doing?' said the man officer.

'She thinks the maggots have got into her clothes,' explained Mum.

'Where are the maggots?' demanded one of the figures in the hazard suits.

'Upstairs,' said Mum. 'In the first bedroom on the left, and some may have got out on to the landing.'

Krystal glared at me. 'If they've got into my room I shall kill you!' she hissed.

'It's not my fault!' I protested. 'I didn't open the packet!'

The people in hazard suits ran up the stairs holding large bags and cases and what looked like vacuum cleaners.

'This is incredible!' said Paul, awed. 'It's like being in a sci-fi film!'

One of the uniformed police officers's radios crackled into life and a voice said: 'Base to 341, over.'

The man officer triggered his radio and replied: '341 receiving, over.'

'Where are you, 341?' demanded the voice on the radio. 'You're supposed to be here for a meeting with the Superintendent. Over.'

'We're stuck in a house under attack by flesh-eating maggots,' said the police officer. 'Over.'

There was a short silence. Then the voice from the radio said: 'Base to 341. Of all the excuses I've ever heard, that is the stupidest you've ever come up with. If you're not here at the station in fifteen minutes you'll be in big trouble. Over and out.'

The police officer sighed. 'This isn't my day,' he said gloomily.

CHAPTER 24

We all stood in the living room and listened to the noise of the people in the hazard suits crashing around on the landing and in my room. None of us sat down – mainly because we were worried that some of the flesh-eating maggots might have got between the cushions on the settees and chairs. With all of us in that same room it was pretty crowded. It wasn't made any easier with Aunt Dora bashing into everyone as she screeched about the room half-naked, while Uncle Pete tried to calm her down.

'What's going on?'

Dad was standing in the doorway looking baffled.

'How did you get in?' demanded Mum.

'Through the back door,' replied Dad. 'I couldn't

get in the front way because the road's full of police cars and ambulances and fire engines.' He saw Dora and frowned, even more bewildered. 'What's Dora doing without any clothes on?'

'The maggots!' Aunt Dora moaned, and then she gave a shriek which made us all cover our ears.

'I'm sure screaming that loud's an offence,' muttered the woman police officer.

'Maggots?' repeated Dad, when he'd recovered from Aunt Dora's shriek.

'Yes,' said Mum. 'They were in a package in Dave's wardrobe.'

Dad looked at me. 'So *that's* what happened to them!' he said.

We all stared at him.

'You know about them?' demanded Mum.

'Of course,' said Dad. 'They're *my* maggots.'

It took about another two hours for the fuss to die down. First, Dad had to go upstairs to explain to the people in hazard suits that the maggots that they were trying to collect weren't actually dangerous flesh-eating maggots but just ordinary harmless ones.

They didn't believe him of course. Three of them continued tearing my furniture apart while the fourth made contact with his HQ on his radio.

Finally, one of them compared a maggot he'd captured with a picture in a book he had which contained photographs and diagrams of all different sorts of maggots. When he'd done that, he took his helmet off and snapped at the others: 'All right. False alarm! Back to base!'

He then gave Dad a form to fill in, and told him there might be charges against him for making a false alarm call.

Once Uncle Pete was sure there weren't any real flesh-eating maggots lurking around, he tried to persuade Aunt Dora to go upstairs and put some clothes on. Dora refused to go anywhere. So Mum ordered the rest of us out of the living room while Uncle Pete went up to my room to gather Aunt Dora's clothes and pack her bag. The good news was that Aunt Dora was going home.

As soon as the emergency services had gone, Krystal ran up to her room to phone her friend, Shelly, and tell her everything that had happened. Me, Paul, Mum and Dad went into the kitchen for some explanations.

'A few days ago I ordered some maggots as fishing bait,' said Dad. 'When the maggots didn't arrive I phoned up the company and asked what had happened to them. They said they might have got lost in the post, so they'd send me another lot.'

'So they weren't anything to do with the TV programme?' I asked.

'No,' said Dad. He frowned. 'And if you hadn't

opened a package that wasn't addressed to you, none of this would have happened.'

'But it *was* addressed to me,' I defended myself. 'It had DJ Dickens on the label. Which is me. David James Dickens. Your name is John. John Dickens.'

Dad shook his head. 'Everyone calls me John, but that's really my second name. The name I was given on my birth certificate is Derek John Dickens, and that's the initials on my credit card. Even though I told them to send the maggots to John Dickens, they must have used the initials on the credit card I used to buy them. DJ Dickens.'

Mum gave a huge sigh. 'But why didn't you mention the fact that you'd ordered some maggots that hadn't arrived? Then Dave would have known what these maggots were!'

'Because of Dora,' said Dad, looking surprised that Mum had even asked. 'You know what she's like about creepy crawlies. If I'd even mentioned the word "maggot" when she was around, she'd have started imagining they were crawling all over her.'

'They were!' laughed Paul. 'Seeing her with no clothes on like that ...'

He caught my mum's We Are Not Amused glare and stopped laughing.

'Not that I did!' he said hastily. 'I didn't look!'

Mum kept glaring.

'I'd better get home,' Paul mumbled. 'Mum and Dad will be wondering where I've got to. I'm sorry for all the trouble, Mrs Dickens.'

'It wasn't your fault, Paul,' said Mum, her expression softening. 'You were just being a good friend to Dave.'

As Paul left, Aunt Dora and Uncle Pete appeared from the living room. Aunt Dora now had clothes on again, and Uncle Pete was carrying Aunt Dora's bag.

'Dora says she's coming home with me,' Pete told us cheerfully. 'And we're going to be very happy together.'

'I shall be in therapy over this for years,' moaned Dora, looking not happy at all. 'I have been traumatised. I am still in a state of shock. I shall be seeing maggots everywhere I look.'

'I'm sure you'll soon get over it,' said Mum.

Very firmly she ushered Dora out through the front door. Pete trudged out after her, and Mum shut the door on them both.

'Hurrah!' she said. 'At last we can get back to a normal life.'

CHAPTER 25

The first thing I did was move my stuff back into my room. The second thing I did was check around in case any of the maggots were still hiding in the carpet or behind the furniture so I could put them in my Science collection. But the people in the hazard suits had done a really good job and got rid of them all.

Once everything was back to normal, I went out to Fred's kennel and clipped his lead on his collar.

'Walkies, Fred,' I said.

It was good to be free again and not under house arrest. I had also been worried that Fred might have been upset by all the hullabaloo: the police and the fire engines and the people in the hazard suits and everything. But Fred seemed happy enough.

At the park I let Fred off the lead so he could have a good run. With me not being allowed to take him for walks for the last couple of days, he hadn't got as much exercise as he liked.

I was watching him run around and chase leaves when I felt something hard prod me painfully in the back. I turned – and came face to face with Banger Bates. I could see the boil big and purple and horrible on his forehead.

FACTOID:
Spots and Zits

Spots, or zits, form when the glands in the skin that produce an oily substance called sebum get clogged up. Blackheads turn black because keratin (the stuff hair is made of) builds up in the glands and pushes out the sebum.

'You got me in trouble!' he snarled. 'I'm gonna bash you up.'

After all that I've been through, and I still get

bashed up! I thought in despair.

And then I thought – why should I let myself be bashed up by this idiot? So instead I plucked up my courage and said: 'No.'

Banger stopped as he was about to hit me. 'What?' he said.

'I said no,' I repeated. 'You're not gonna bash me up. Because if you do I shall hit your boil and it

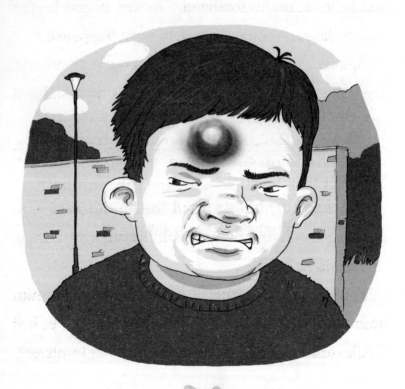

will burst and you'll get blood poisoning and die.'

Banger didn't answer at once. I could almost see his brain trying to work. Finally he said in accusing tones: 'You told me those maggots were maggots that ate people. They weren't. They were just ordinary maggots. Because of you I got told off by my dad for making him look stupid.'

'No,' I said. 'You got into trouble because you stole those maggots from my locker. If you hadn't taken them, none of this would have happened.'

Banger stood glaring and scowling at me, clenching and unclenching his fists as he wondered what to do. Finally he decided.

'I don't care,' he snapped. 'I'm gonna bash you up anyway!'

And with that he grabbed me by the shirt with one big hand, and pulled back his other in a huge fist ready to belt me.

A deep growling sound behind Banger made him stop. Fred was standing there with his lips pulled back and his very sharp teeth showing, a terrible vengeful growl coming out of his throat.

'Remember Fred?' I said, as calmly as I could.

Oh yes. Banger remembered Fred all right. Fred had chased him and his mates right out of the park once when they'd been threatening me.

'As you know,' I continued as Banger hesitated, 'he will leap on you and tear off bits of your flesh if you hit me. And that'll be much more painful than any maggots could ever be.'

Banger still stood there, holding me on my tiptoes. Fred jerked towards him, growling even more. Letting go of me, Banger leapt back in alarm. Unfortunately for him, he stepped into a big poo that Fred had just done and slipped over, landing right on his bum in the middle of the stinky brown pile.

'Urgh! Gross!' Banger yelled, a look of pure disgust on his face as he struggled to get back on to his feet.

'If you hadn't been threatening me, I would have picked that up in a proper poo bag,' I told him.

'Now you'll just have to go home and wipe it off.'

I gave a short whistle to Fred, who stepped over the fallen Banger to join me. As he passed Banger, he farted. It got Banger right in the face.

'Aaargh!' moaned Banger, and collapsed, his head falling backwards on to another piece of dog poo that I hadn't noticed before.

I clipped Fred's lead back on. 'Come on, Fred,' I said. 'Let's go home.'

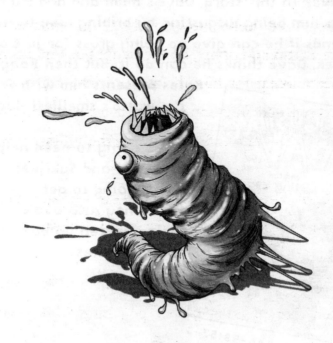

and the
farting dog

Why not get your hands on another book about Dave? In this story, Dave's mum and dad try to stop him being disgusting by bribing him: twenty pounds if he can give up being gross for just one week. Dave thinks he can do it. But then Banger Bates presents him with Fred: the world's smelliest dog.

Dave's going to need help from Paul and Sukijeet if he's going to get his money AND avoid being beaten up by Banger Bates...

978-0-340-98157-3